Praise for Baffling Year One

"There are no false notes in this strange and dazzling anthology of 26 queer, speculative stories, selected from the first year of *Baffling Magazine*—which is particularly impressive given the wide range of tone, subject matter, and subgenre."

—Publishers Weekly (starred review)

Neon Hemlock Press
www.neonhemlock.com
@neonhemlock

© Stories copyrighted 2022-2023
© 2024 for anthology as a whole

Baffling Year Three
edited by dave ring, Craig L. Gidney & Gabriella Etoniru

All rights reserved. No part of this publication may be reproduced, stored in a retrieval system or transmitted in any form or by any means, electronic, mechanical, photocopying, recording or otherwise without the prior permission of the publisher or in accordance with the provisions of the Copyright, Designs and Patents Act 1988 or under the terms of any licence permitting limited copying issued by the Copyright Licensing Agency.

Cover Illustration by Carly A-F
Cover Design by dave ring
Interior Design and Layout by dave ring
Interior Harpy Illustrations by Robin Ha

Print ISBN-13: 978-1-952086-96-0
Ebook ISBN-13: 978-1-952086-97-7

edited by dave ring, Craig L. Gidney & Gabriella Etoniru
BAFFLING YEAR THREE

Neon Hemlock Press

NEON HEMLOCK

Baffling
Year Three

EDITED BY DAVE RING
CRAIG L. GIDNEY & GABRIELLA ETONIRU

ASSOCIATE EDITORS
D. A. VOROBYOV, ATHAR FIKRY
& AUN-JULI RIDDLE

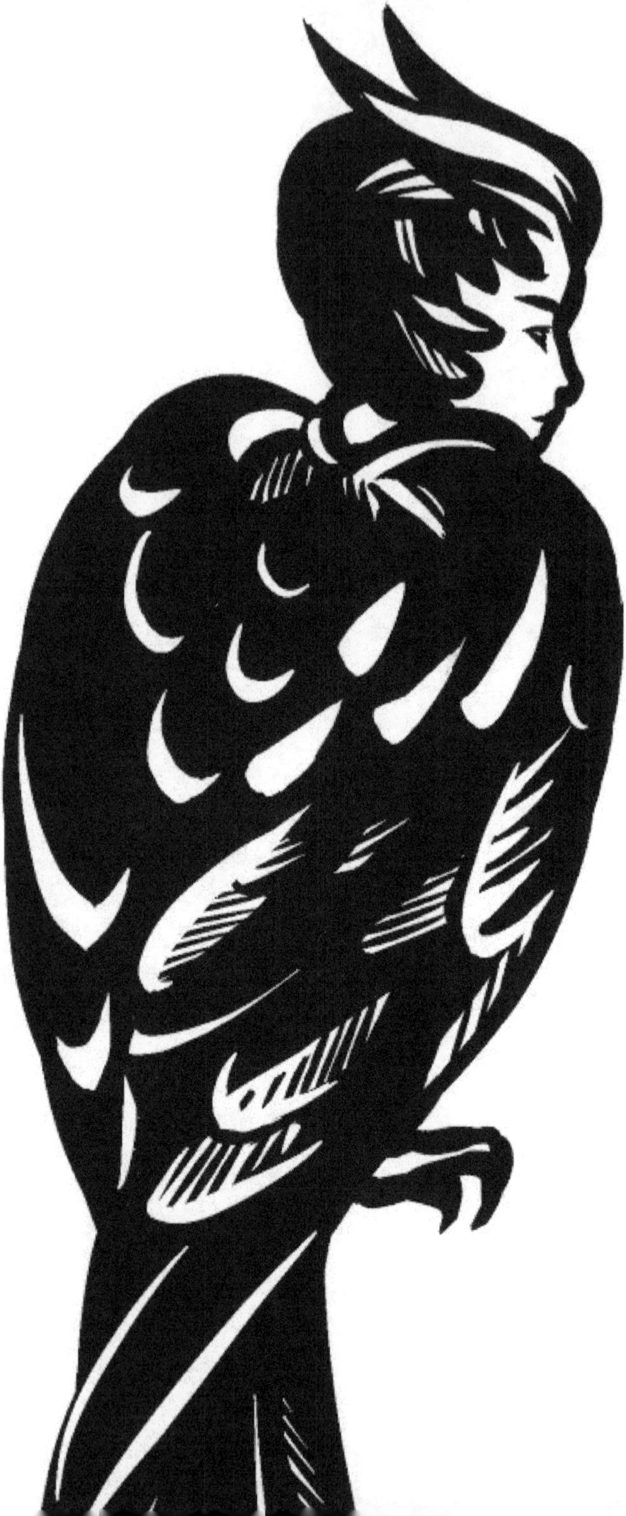

SPECULATIVE

Flash

Fiction

with a

Queer

Bent

A Letter from One of the Editors

We've reached three years of *Baffling Magazine*, and the spectrum of queer experience dispayed in these pages is as broad and beautiful as ever, from love keening through the ocean depths to a yearning fit for the stars.

This anthology contains the first of our intentionally themed issues, Food (Issue Ten) and Fashion (Issue Twelve), and those stories will find you naked and hungry and leave you warm and fed. Wear your sharpest eyeliner, brew your best dress, or find something a little cozier—whatever makes you feel most comfortable—we're taking you to dinner. Devoted grilled cheese sandwiches, whispers and biscuits, and nostalgic strawberries are just a taste of this delicious menu, and we won't be held responsible if you're left wanting more (but we'll comply if asked and eagerly offer you more delectable fictional morsels)!

These stories, themed and unthemed, resonated with our editors in ways both comforting and unexpected. They helped us find parts of ourselves—unearthed feelings, memories, moments previously hidden. All the more important at a time when we sometimes find our communities fractured or our friends distant, when we are longing for connection. These authors have written words to link us together, however vast the space (and time) between us may be.

Whatever it is you're looking for in life or fiction, we hope here you find something *memorable* or *haunting* or *simply delicious*.

Aun-Juli Riddle
Baltimore, June 2024

Issue Nine

The Blade, The Hammer by Lina Rather	1
From the Mothers That Swam Before by Marisca Pichette	5
Nine in Number by E. Catherine Tobler	9
Approximation and Displacement by Portia Elan	11
What Are We if I Stay by K.S. Walker	13
With Open Eyes by Nikolas Sky	19
An Absent Presence by Alice Pow	23
Despair, Divided by Tamara Jerée	27
How the Wolf Domesticated Herself by December Cuccaro	31

Issue Ten

Prix Fixe Menu by Aimee Ogden	35
What You Want Before You Know It by Matt Terl	39
An Unsound Heart by R.S. Saha	47
They Commune With the Dead Using Biscuit Crumbs and Wine by Elou Carroll	53
Turducken by Lindz McLeod	55
Icariana by Wen-yi Lee	63
It's Just a Date by A. Tony Jerome	67

Contents

Issue Eleven

The Little Free Guide To Dronewatching, Abridged & Annotated by Ann LeBlanc	71
The Flame Without by Tarver Nova	77
A Practical Study of Time by M.P. Rosalia	83
All the Things I Could've Done That Wouldn't Have Been So Devastating by Phoebe Barton	89
You Who Does Not Exist by Aigner Loren Wilson	93
'Sup, Handsome? by Sharang Biswas	97
How to Stay Married to Baba Yaga by S.M. Hallow	113

Issue Twelve

I Want To Wear You Like A Glove by Anneke Schwob	119
Darn by Mary Sanche	123
Evergreen by Megan Baffoe	127
Call Me, Said Kali In Her Black Modified YSLs by Akira Leong	131
Aristophanes Airs His Dirty Laundry by Bastian Hart	133
Of Available Materials by Tianran Li-Harkness	139
Grown Gown by Derek Des Anges	143

Contributors	*148*
About the Magazine / About the Press	*156*

The Blade, The Hammer

Lina Rather

"I'm sorry about your aunt," Mia said. Beside her on the fallen log, Sanan scrubbed her toe in the dirt and scowled at the dust she kicked up. They'd come back here to escape the noise and grease of Mia's father's smithy, but now the silence hung just as weighty as the racket of bellows and hammers.

"I didn't really know her," Sanan said. "She was always off in the capital, being a hero. Dying a hero." Suddenly she grabbed Mia's hand and squeezed it tight, and like every furtive time they'd held hands, Mia's heart skipped beneath her ribs. Fourteen was too young to be in love, everyone told them. Fourteen was too young to do anything adult.

Or it had been, until last week when Sanan's aunt died, and Sanan woke the next morning with the glyph of the great protector glowing on her hand. Fourteen was not, apparently, too young for Sanan to be chosen by the implacable and unknowable powers of the kingdom. It wasn't even supposed to be her. She had six cousins downriver in the capital, all trained in combat and sorcery since birth by the finest tutors. But the inheritance running in her family's blood cared nothing for any of that, it seemed.

Mia felt the growing calluses on Sanan's hand from her new weapons training. "Is it going to be heavy, do you think?" Sanan asked. Once she went to the capital, those calluses would harden until she stopped noticing the grit of the hilt. The thought that someday soon Sanan's touch would feel like a stranger's hit Mia straight in the center of her chest. "You know how I hate carrying water back from the well."

"Dad's making you a small one first." The only swords they'd played with before were crudely carved planks of wood. When they were smaller and still silly, they ran in a pack with the other village children, smacking each other around until someone hit too hard and drew blood and all their mothers came out to yell at them. "And they'll train you to carry it. You'll have glorious muscles."

In the village square, the adults were decking the houses with wreaths and pennants and streamers. Someone was making a cake, someone else was roasting a whole baby hog. What a great honor for them that the land's magic had chosen one of their own.

Mia swallowed. The smithy smoke burned the back of her throat. Or she told herself it was the smoke. If the world blurred under a film of tears? Just the soot stinging her eyes.

"We'll write," Sanan said. "You'll write me, won't you?"

"Of course." Now it was her turn to squeeze Sanan's hand.

"And if I die, you'll come see me? Lying in state?"

"You're not going to *die*."

"You don't know that." And now Sanan's eyes shone, and she used her other hand, the branded one, to wipe the traitorous tears away. "Lots of people die in war. Even people with magic. They won't keep me in training forever."

Mia tried to breathe, but it was like someone had her in their grip, crumpling her up. She couldn't cry now, not when Sanan needed her. This morning, she'd crept in through Mia's bedroom window and curled against her on the narrow mattress until her tears had soaked the pillow. Mia's own would have to wait until Sanan had ridden off, dressed in the imperial blue she was now permitted to wear.

She didn't want this. This moment was the first forever-thing in her life and every time she thought of the weight of *forever*, it felt like dying. She wanted to be a child again, swinging sticks and believing war was nothing more than another story.

"Listen to me," Mia said, as the hiss of steam came from the smithy. "You'll go to the capital and learn to be the best swordmaster in the kingdom and the war will end before your training does. You'll be safe." It tumbled out of her all at once, like she was speaking a future into being. "We'll write each other every day. You'll be so beautiful in your armor that I'll dream of you in it every night. And my father will teach me his craft, so that every time you break a sword, I can be the one to make you a new one."

Sanan was crying silently now, looking out into the setting sun on the horizon. Mia kissed her hair and tried to remember all of this, the sun and Sanan's face and the warmth in the space between them.

Then the wide door to the smithy flew open, and there was her father, a thin and shining sword in his hand. He held it out, even though he was a hundred yards away. It would be, Mia knew, the best thing he had ever made.

Sanan stood, and let go of Mia's hand, and went to accept her inheritance.

From the Mothers That Swam Before

Marisca Pichette

To the woman who braids kelp at the bottom of the sea:
I hear you singing every night. Songs you learned from the whales, passed down through waves—generations diving, seeking the darkest places to fill with sound.

I see you crowned in urchins, kelp encasing your arms and pooling in your lap. I see your iridescence: aquamarine and crimson and that scar just below your left gill. You were attacked by a sailfish while swimming alone. You swim nowhere now.

Your eyes are pale; they've forgotten how sunlight feels.

I see the shard of propeller, too, still embedded in your tail. Whorls of scales flash as you float, as you sink. Under all the waves the sea still moves you with its pulse. You let it, buried in kelp and shadow.

Most of all, I see the blanket you are braiding. It fills the water around you, fills the cave that must be something like the place you hatched, when you swam your first strokes in lighter waves. Brown and green and black, your work eddies like a life apart, your only company in the depths.

I wonder why you dove, leaving coral and light behind. You spent the best years of your life with dolphins, yet they do not visit you in your cave at the foot of the world. Did you lose them in clouded currents? Were they beside you when the propeller struck, left you limping down to the personless depths? I have seldom known a pod to abandon one of its own. Had you been among seals, things could have been different.

Yet we never dive as deep as your cave.

You alone produce no light, eels bioluminescing between the loose white strands of your hair. I see them, too—lighting your work. Though after years you have learned to braid without sight, your hardened fingers finding their way.

Alone with your craft, you hum the tunes of the whales.

Once a sperm whale found you, drawn to your keening, absent-minded song. She loved your curious accent, the lilting melody she recalled from her calfhood. At the mouth of your cave, she brought you news of stars and seagulls. She told you of shapes she saw in the clouds and gossip she shared with orcas.

She urged you, politely, to rejoin the lighter sea. She feared for the future you'd find, isolated in darkness as no mermaid should live.

You declined. Kelp in your hands, white in your hair, you stayed in aloneness.

She honored your decision, though she worried when she left. As a parting gesture, she brought you a colossal squid to eat. You might yet have some left, each meal a practice of groping sensation in the lightless depths.

I wonder—what will you do when the squid runs out? What will you do when your hands fumble for kelp, and there is none more to braid? Will you be content to remain as you are, in those coldest waves?

Or will you raise your face at last, and sing?

†

IN MY MIND'S eye, you rest on a carpet of kelp, braiding with webbed and wrinkled hands. Your arms trail jellyfish tentacles and your hair glimmers with treasures brought to you by crabs. In my mind you are beautiful and gray.

You do not see or hear me, in your cave at the bottom of the sea. You do not wonder how I wear my hair, or what wrought the wrinkles under my eyes.

I wear my hair in a braid when I am on land. In the sea, though, I let it loose. The wrinkles I harvested from the wind, from salt and cold. I wonder if yours were carved by waves.

You do not know me at all. You do not know that I, too, learned to sing from the whales. Into their music I weave my own seal songs, inherited from my mother and her mother and the mothers that swam before.

I like to imagine that we were singing the same song, when the sperm whale found us. You in your cave, me in the bay—diving as rain turned the waves rough.

She rose from the dark, humming music we both know. Music we both sing with accents borne from the waters that birthed us.

Circling a school of hake, she told me about you.

Alone at the bottom of the sea, you think no one can see you. No one can hear you. But I can. In my mind you braid and sing and drift. Before I shed my coat and came ashore, rain washing the salt from my skin, I asked her to follow your song a second time.

I gave her a message. I know she will not forget a single word.

†

IF YOU EVER TIRE of the depths, if your fingertips grow cold and numb between kelp leaves—sing the song of the sperm whale.

She will find you. Take her tail in your rough hands, and hold tight.

I will be waiting in the bay, my hair loose and my voice thrown to the waves. Where our songs meet, let go. You won't sink; the seals will catch you.

When our hands intertwine, I will see you at last outside of my mind. You will hear me outside of her voice. Between waves and rocks, neither of us need drift alone.

My coat can keep us both warm.

NINE IN NUMBER

E. Catherine Tobler

A trail of nine freckles curls down the shadow of your spine, some so small they might not be counted as proper at all, but I count them, one by one by one, with fingers and lips and tongue.

It will change everything, you say. Your back arches under my firm kiss on the fifth freckle, this near the curve of your waist. This freckle tastes like salt.

Yes, everything, I say, and slide lower, counting the freckles aloud. *But maybe nothing,* I add, your fingers moving through my loose hair, a fist and then fingers blossoming open when you can't hold on, have to let go because you always let me go in the end. What if I let the intel go? What if we stayed on our side of the galaxy? What if we stopped counting other worlds and focused on our own?

Your mother—

I don't want to talk about my mother.

Her blood is no longer on my hands, but some nights I feel it. Tonight, I don't, only because you're in my hands and I'm counting freckles and not potential planets. I can't see my mother sprawled on the ground, her life's blood spreading blue as oxygen sparks color into it, into the documents she killed for. The documents I also killed for.

Do you...

You trail off and I lift my head. I know what you're going to ask, your eyes shining like eclipsed moons in the half-light that falls over my bed.

Do I believe the scientists' findings? Yes. My mother would not have killed if she didn't believe in it—wouldn't have killed to cover it up if she didn't believe that life existed beyond this world we know. It terrified her, that life could do that—be something we couldn't control, but how can you control anything? Can you control the way you feel when my tongue slides past that ninth freckle?

Nine freckles like the nine smudges of light they pulled from the night skies; nine dreams, nine hopes. Maybe eight, they argued—one is so very small and distant and impossible. Only one lingers in the zone of habitability, only one gleams vaguely blue and green even at this vast distance. Oxygen and nitrogen and warmth and liquid water and maybe, maybe life.

My fingers slide down over your belly, over the life that may even now spread within you.

They will know I killed her, they will know she killed the others; she smashed their telescopes, and meant to burn their research, but I couldn't allow that, could I? Not if I mean to rule in ways my mother never did.

I don't have to ask you; we've had this conversation before, and you won't stop me. You won't stop me from walking out that door in the morning and telling the world what they found, what she tried to cover up, what I killed to reveal.

You won't stop me. But sometimes, oh how I wish you would.

Approximation and Displacement

Portia Elan

Someone's great-aunt dies. Someone buys a star in memory of her great-aunt: you know, the mail-order star-naming schemes that come with a coordinate map and little certificate sealed by the American Astronomical Society, Inc, which are a delight to space-minded and poetic children and the sentimental among us.

Someone buys a star and names it Kim after her great-aunt and she stands sometimes (but not every night) outside her Missouri house and tries to use the coordinate map to find Kim somewhere in the sky. She ignores the ordinary ways that human Kim is still there, in the towering pecan trees, the persistent tulips, the musty curtains (who could be bothered to wash curtains?) and seven lipsticks—all *Love That Red*. Kim is still there in a list of phone numbers with spidery handwriting listing "niece," "sister," "cousin," "neighbor," beside each name, and the barest of checkmarks on each line, as though Kim wanted to keep track: who called, and who did not. One name with no room beside it because every day there was a call. Every day a voice on the other end of the line.

Someone buys a star and names it Kim and does not confirm that the star is still alive, does not ask if the star has its own name. She peers up at the sky and wishes the lights of the town nearby were quieter—what a funny word to use for light—so she could see the stars better. The star named Kim is alive. The star named Kim is a sun around which turns a scattering of planets—some gas, some liquid, one something like Earth, although not Earth. It is enough to say that the planet was something like Earth.

When the name Kim arrives at the star, the star's gravity changes. Is it really gravity that changes? That is close enough. The star named Kim's gravity changes and so changes the planet that is like Earth. Beneath the surface, bulbs grow thick and in the spring break the dirt with their thirsty, soft mouths. They are persistent. A fungus, bright as *Love That Red*, unfurls across the rocky shores of the seas.

Someone's great-aunt dies and, packing Kim's home—where she lived for seventy-six years—someone discovers a name on a list of family: a name she has never seen before. Evie—and instead of "cousin" or "neighbor" (no "daughter" or "son" or "husband" to be found on the list), next to Evie is the word "heart."

Someone's great aunt dies and she buys a star and names it Kim, and when the star hears the name Kim, it turns and turns and burns and cries out to the universe in search of a star named Evie.

WHAT ARE WE IF I STAY

K.S. Walker

It has been three weeks, six days and seven hours since Georgia disappeared through the door. The one carved from mist that sometimes hangs between the two dogwood trees. Esme stares at the spot through her kitchen window. This time of year the dogwoods are crowned with soft white petals. Last June, Esme and Georgia spread a checkered blanket beneath the flowering branches and fed each other strawberries and slices of Honeycrisps topped with curls of aged gouda. Today, her stomach curdles to look at the spot. But she cannot bring herself to look at the folded note she is holding, either.

†

It was Esme who saw the door first. It appeared late morning in the slushy in-between time when Spring tries to wrest itself from Winter. They stood together, Esme cradled against Georgia's chest, trying to figure out what the door could mean. It was gone before their coffee cooled.

It was Georgia who kept the notebook. When the door appeared. Under what conditions. How long it stayed. There was no pattern as far as either of them could tell.

Esme is observant: she saw the eager shining in Georgia's eyes whenever the door appeared, the way that Georgia withdrew in the days following its disappearance. But Esme never thought it would come to this.

†

ONE WEEK AFTER Georgia left, Esme stopped sleeping in their bed. It was too painful to wake up in the middle of the night clutching cold sheets in the spot where Georgia should have been. Instead, she made a spot for herself on the couch each evening, thinking of what Georgia might write in the note that would surely come—she said she'd send word as soon as she was able. Each morning Esme rolled her quilt and pillow back up and placed them on a high shelf in the hall closet, certain that today would be the day.

†

TWO WEEKS AFTER Georgia left, the door appeared again. Esme was drying dishes and in between putting away a glass and reaching for a plate—there it was—the door spanned the distance between the dogwoods that framed it, its pointed archway lost to their thickening canopy. A dish slipped from Esme's grasp and shattered.

An anxious pump of adrenaline spiked in her stomach and settled in her throat. The room spun, and Esme's breaths came too close together. She leaned her weight into the counter until the edge bit against her palms. She focused on the crunch of the broken plate beneath her houseshoes. The plink of water dripping in the faucet.

Her vision cleared and she went outside to wait.

Esme waited until the sun was a sliver of burnished gold at the treeline. She waited until fireflies began their flickering dance across the yard. Even as the hope that was sustaining her slowed to a trickle and was replaced with grief as bottomless as the summer days are long, she waited. The moon rose heavy and bright and Esme made her bed once again in the living room, alone.

†

TODAY, SHE HOLDS a note. It is written on a large heart-shaped leaf with scalloped edges. The leaf is thin and pliable enough to have been folded in half without cracking. Esme found it on her front porch pinned beneath a rock. The sparrows that live in the bushes on either side of the front door ceased their morning twittering as she bent to pick it up. Esme sits at her kitchen table and unfolds the leaf. The note does not say: *The stars here remind me of your smile, the air of the soft scent I only find when I bury my face between your neck and shoulder. I miss you. I'll be home soon.*

The note also does not say: *I can now say I have explored another world only to discover that which I already knew; there is no one on this earth or beyond that compares to you.*

Instead, Esme runs a trembling finger down flaking letters—she has a dark suspicion—and reads: *The maples cant be trusted! Unsure about birds. DO NOT FOLLOW.*

With Open Eyes

Nikolas Sky

The thing in the garden never was a magnolia tree. Adelio said it was, and it was similar in a lot of ways: the broad, oval leaves that angled to a point. The cup-shaped buds of the tulip variety. The lean, elegant branches.

But magnolias don't have black bark, and even black tulip magnolias don't have blood-red flowers.

I spent three years working for Adelio before I saw him in person. Three years of tending to his borders of begonia rex, Persian Violet cyclamen, blue sweet pea, and white heather. Of shaping the delicate oleander bushes and trimming the pale pink tea roses that made up the border of his dark, grand manor.

When I saw the first hint of flowers in the "magnolia" tree, it had been almost three years to the day. I left Adelio a note under the front door, smudged with soil, letting him know they would be opening soon. True magnolias can take up to a decade to flower; I thought he would want to see it.

Three days later, he was simply *there* when I turned around. Lean and darkly beautiful in a black suit, with long, thick black hair. He belonged among the flowers as much as I did the dirt. His visible eye—the other covered by a patch—was a startling lavender.

"Call me Adelio," he said, while I was trying to remember my words. "Your work around my home has been astounding, Mister Reed."

I involuntarily crushed the cut leaves I held. "Sil." I licked dry lips. "Sil's fine. Your garden's great. The magnolia...I've never seen anything like it."

He smiled; an ache blossomed in my chest. "A truly special one; the Wide-Eyed Magnolia. You will see why when the flowers open."

I followed him closer to the tree.

"It blooms so rarely," he said, caressing one of the dark branches fondly. "In just a few weeks, you'll see something truly striking."

†

I ATTENDED TO the tree anxiously after that, trimming away the tiniest hint of a dead leaf or discolored bark. The vivid blossoms grew slowly, soft even to my coarse fingers. I swore they whispered when I touched the branches. No discernable words, but they tickled the back of my mind. I wanted to understand.

Days later, as I was finishing work, I found Adelio by the tree, smoothing dirt around the roots with the back of a spade. He knelt on the ground with his back to me, and didn't so much as glance back. "Good afternoon, Sil. No, I am not dissatisfied with your work. I simply enjoy giving our friend a little treat from time to time."

"How did you know that I was here?" And for that matter, exactly what I was thinking.

"The tree told me," he said pleasantly.

Of course the tree would tell him. In any other situation, I would think him mad, but why would it not whisper to him as it did to me? I stood beside him and looked up. The flowers were full and heavy, looking all the more like blood against the dark branches. "They should be opening any day now."

Three days.

"Three days," I repeated.

Adelio rose, dusting his knees off before cleaning his hands on a towel. "I have been waiting so long for this, and I've given so much for its care. You will be here, won't you? I know that it's your day off, but you must see the moment they open."

"Of course," I said. "This tree...I want to see the mystery it holds. The secrets within the flowers."

"It has many mysteries, as anything beautiful does."

"Then you must have a thousand mysteries." I froze. "I'm sorry, I shouldn't—"

Adelio smiled. "Will you come inside with me, Sil?"

My eyes flicked away from his face. "I'm dirty."

"Nothing grows without dirt."

What had he buried beneath the tree? The possibilities buzzed inside of my brain.

Go inside.

I nodded to Adelio. "I...I will, but please, let me wash up."

"Of course. I will make us tea."

I washed my hands and face under icy water from the spigot outside, and then entered, shivering. The inside of the house was as grand as the outside: dark woods, lush fabrics, and bold paintings of trees of the like I'd never seen.

He found me examining one such painting and touched my shoulder; his lavender eye was as unearthly and alluring as the tree we both cared for.

I cannot say who moved in for a kiss first, but our arms were soon around each other, and the tea went cold.

The next morning, I crept out of the house and gently dug around the tree's roots to see what Adelio had buried.

I saw nothing.

†

THE NIGHT BEFORE the tree bloomed, an unseasonal frost came. I dressed and raced to the house without so much as shaving, afraid of the flowers freezing and dying.

Adelio was already standing before it. "Come here, Sil," he said, white curling up from his mouth, and held his hand out to me.

I squeezed his fingers between mine and stared at the tree. As if it had been waiting for me, the petals of every blossom parted, curling back to proudly display their heart: an eye in each, all turning to look at me.

I stopped breathing.

"We are connected," Adelio said, looking at the blossoms lovingly. "An eye is a small price to pay for such beauty, don't you think?"

"A small price to pay," I echoed, awed.

Adelio cradled my cheek against his palm. "You could stay here with me, the two of us tending it and the rest of the garden. Would you like that, Sil?"

Please, Sil.

I put my hand over his. "I would like nothing more," I whispered.

"I can retrieve a knife," Adelio said, but I stopped him with a shake of my head.

"The tree needs to feel this."

Adelio covered his mouth with his hand, then let it drop. "Oh, Sil, you *do* understand."

I plunged my fingers into my right socket. Through the hot rush of blood, the eyes watched us, unblinking and stunningly lavender. I had never seen anything so perfect.

I ripped my eye free like an uprooted weed. Even as my knees buckled from the pain and I collapsed into Adelio's arms, I held my sacrifice aloft like a prize. Soon, I would be connected, too.

Ten years could not come soon enough.

An Absent Presence

Alice Pow

The golf cart buckles as I pull off the asphalt and onto dead grass. It buckles again as we climb back onto asphalt. The parking lot opens to the road on the other side, but there's nothing stopping us from a little shortcut.

I stash the keys under the brake while Lauren crushes a cigarette under her sandal. She hops out of the cart, but I stare ahead, thoughts hazy and unpronounceable.

She taps my arm. "Let's go."

I follow her and together we wander between grey cabins. The houses on the river belong to people who don't even live here. Vacation homes for retired, heterosexual couples who pay almost no property taxes so they do nothing for the local economy and infrastructure.

The rest of the town is usually empty. The pub, the barbershop, the grocery store. Everything is just peeling plaster and unpaved roads. Nothing much to do for a pair of twenty-year-olds bored out of our minds.

So we try to keep our minds off the feelings we can't express. Those wordless gnawing things that challenge our limited vocabulary for what the hell anything makes us feel like.

A few times each summer, we take a break from getting plastered in Lauren's basement to go swimming in the Mississippi. We'll get in the water and swim out to a sandbank a couple-hundred feet away.

My parents sell and rent out golf carts, and even though I'm not allowed to take them wherever, Mom says it's fine if we're just going to the river.

She doesn't know I'm dating Lauren or that I'm gay. It's a miracle Lauren and I know it about ourselves. For the longest time it was another absent presence neither of us had the tools to understand.

Hopefully, some day, the two of us can get the hell out of here and never look back.

What I like about the river is that it looks weightless and heavy at the same time. On some level, I know that tons of water is heavy and forceful, but watching it, so quick and constant, I have to believe it weighs nothing, right?

Lauren takes my hand and kisses me on the shoulder. The sun peeks through the sky as clouds move across it like tectonic plates. The air is still except for the fucking gnats everywhere.

"Haven't I given these things enough of my blood?" I ask.

"That's the problem. You're a staple of their diet at this point," Lauren says. As she walks, she kicks off her sandals and picks them up without missing a beat. "Your blood is essential to their ecosystem."

As we walk between the cabins, I hold Lauren's hand for a dangerous moment as fear bites my ankles. When we come out on the other side, something's wrong.

The river *is not*. An error message like from a shitty old computer *is*. It reads *Server Maintenance May Cause Outages. Please, Standby.*

What does that even mean? The message encompasses the whole river, a grey box stretching endlessly in either direction, but it's not there at the same time. It *is* but not here, I guess. This new absent presence gnashes the underside of my skin.

The sandbank still *is* across the way but the texture of the sand looks pixelated and clunky even from a distance.

Lauren's face stays blank like she doesn't know how to process; I know mine is too. A nothing in our heads bites and bleeds. We are clipping through the intended programming. Even that thought *is* absent-present. It crowds all available space in my head, numb and intense like an opioid migraine. Like teeth so sharp there's no words for it.

Another pop up arrives with a harsh ding: *The Application* **Existential Crisis** *has stopped unexpectedly* with a single button to Force Close the program.

Another ding and this one says Do you want to allow this app to make changes to your device? Below that it reads *Program name:* **transcendental crisis** */ File origin: Unknown* plus two buttons for *Yes* and *No*.

Lauren and I both intuit that we are not supposed to see these things. But we have no functions intended for the inputs, so we continue ahead like everything is fine.

I wade through the error, my body bouncing to the bottom of the river and then ten feet in the air until I'm back to the wordlessness. I breathe. Maybe the water hasn't loaded. Lauren is sideways, her arms stretched and twisted in directions they shouldn't go. Algorithmically, we float, swimming-glitching through it all.

"Maybe we should go," I say, and when I try to say things I don't have words for a gap catches in my throat. "���. ��"

"Why?" Lauren asks as her head stretches into the sky. "Is something wrong?"

Another wordless gnawing. More razor sharp teeth in my head. I want to tell her that everything is wrong. I want to tell her the truth.

I try to say it, try to load the thoughts into the hardware of my mouth and throat. I say, "������ �nothing���."

We spend the day there. We go through the motions and then we both go home. Maybe things will change tomorrow.

Despair, Divided

Tamara Jerée

Arcane grips my horn implants, maintaining eye contact as ve guides me down to the bed. I'm flattered that ve's taken on a corporeal form just for me. Arcane says ve knows how humans couple (*couple*—ve is, in fact, an old old god) and asks if that's what I'd like from this experience. (Ve calls it an experience too.) I say I want whatever ve will give someone like me—someone tossed out of their home in the upper city and forced to make a life underground. Someone who knows the shitty metal in their body will one day give them cancer but collects mods like trophies anyway. I'm afraid to ask why ve's chosen me—afraid to ruin a good thing or else acknowledge a bad one while it still feels good.

In this form, Arcane has a head, and ve tilts it at my words. "So we are both fallen, in our own ways."

"What were you the god of?" I ask.

Arcane traces my mods as ve thinks: hand pausing at the patches of black scales on my shoulders, the spines down my back. Ve presses a finger into my mouth and finds steel-plated fangs. "Loss, despair," ve answers distractedly.

Ver words settle heavy and cold. "As in…you brought despair?"

"I removed the despair of others into myself."

I relax. There is so much despair in Lower Providence. "You mean you took those feelings away?"

"Yes."

"Was that…" I don't know how to talk to a god. I didn't know they existed until recently. I lick my lips and catch my tongue on the point of a fang, something I haven't done in years. My mouth tastes like metal as I say, "It sounds like a nice thing to do for people."

Take my despair. Take it. The plea leaps to my mind, unbidden.

At that, Arcane finally returns my gaze—if it could be considered that. Ve has voids where ver eyes should be, but somehow I know ve's regarding me more closely. I realize, perhaps, that ve heard my thoughts as a prayer. If so, it was my first.

"I can give you bodily pleasure," ve says, ver tone haunted by something like regret. "That will have to suffice."

"Yeah, 'course," I say. I lick my lips bloody.

How do you make love to a god of despair? I wonder, even as it happens. There are things one can't say. I couldn't beg for ver to fill me, as ve is empty—the fissures in ver gray skin revealing the nothingness within. I couldn't breathe against ver neck and whisper how much I wanted ver body—for it was not a body but a hollow and temporary vessel. Ve seems aware of this—in ver first tentative touches, in ver questioning glances. Ve seems braced for a look that would betray my repulsion of ver form, then softens when it never appears.

"I want you to pin me down," I say.

Ve does, and they weigh nothing and everything. They are the condensed hopelessness in my chest. They are the numbness that follows tears. I gasp at the sensation.

Ve releases me as if worried I'm hurt. I hold them—as if my mortal body could do anything against a force so deep and old. Ve kisses me. My tongue quests into ver mouth and it too is empty. When ve withdraws, I realize I'm crying.

"I warned you of this," ve says.

I huff and swipe at my eyes. I shove a strap-on harness at ver. Ve seems baffled by the neon dildo.

"Fuck me," I say, throat still tight.

"Only if you are—happy." Ve stumbles into the last word.

"Are you happy?" I counter.

Ve laughs with ver mouth closed.

In another moment, perhaps it might be comical: Arcane—with ver gray skin and lank black hair and void eyes—sporting a jutting pink dildo. But the anticipation of fucking a god would make anyone breathless.

†

ARCANE DOESN'T LEAVE when we're done. Ve looms by my bedside, studying me with ver eyeless gaze. I decide to give ver a pass on ver lack of etiquette. Ve is old. Maybe ve's new to this hooking up thing.

"Do you…often have sex with humans?" I ask.

"You're the only one."

That makes me sit up. "Why me?"

"You remind me of someone from the old days. Someone I was close to."

"Are they not around anymore?"

Arcane returns to the bed, hovering just over the sheets. "How is your despair?" ve asks.

"You mean to ask how I'm feeling," I correct.

"Yes." Ve traces from my horn to my chin. If an eyeless gaze can be tender, this is it. "How are you feeling?"

In the void I see my own emptiness reflected back. I find a grim triumph in the observation: here, at my lowest, a god looks upon me. Even in the dark, I can touch the divine.

My smile bares my fangs. Arcane's answer is my second prayer, a conjuring of what could be—for me, for us both.

How the Wolf Domesticated Herself

December Cuccaro

M‌Y MOTHER SAID never go near men; they only want you for your coat. She took me close to the village where I met a man's gaze from across his fire and recognized his hunger—and something else I couldn't place in my youth, that I now know as hate.

My mother was wrong—they wanted more. My mate—sly, mischievous, unheeding of my warnings—became white teeth ripped from death-paled gums for a necklace, blood spilled to bind her spirit to a knife, lean meat dripping over a fire, cracked bones sucked dry of marrow and discarded in the sluggish embers at the end of the night, and finally, a coat, dappled in every color of the deep winter, stretched thin on a rack. I watched from where the tree's shadows touched the village fields as the man gave it to his mate, who wore my love's face over her own. It didn't fit, but snagged and lumped oddly, the way a rabbit's skull looked after I crushed it in my jaws.

When the hunter ventured into the forest again, I killed him. There would be no second coat, not from a wolf. I wanted to see my mate again, and so once I had eaten his steaming innards, I slipped into his skin. It fit awkwardly;

I was not as precise with my teeth as he'd been with his cutting. I pawed the knife forged with my mate's blood at his hip—my hip— and wondered if I kept it close enough, would I hear her song emanating from it? I wanted was to taste her scent again, sun-warmed and oak-heavy.

I returned to the village late at night when none might remark on my unsteady two-legged gait or the snarl in my long teeth. The woman was asleep, still wrapped in my mate. She shifted into wakefulness as I stood over her. Beneath the coat she was soft and pink like the newborn mice we ate in spring.

Gentle, she said. I didn't know what she meant. When I said nothing, she turned away from me, curled into herself. I took the knife made from my lover's blood and tucked it under the bedding. I wrapped around the curve of her back, dug clumsy fingers into the fur and breathed in deep. She smelled like the wolf she'd been, though I also smelled the woman inside her. She stiffened beneath my touch but didn't shy away, and still buried against her I slept the wary half-sleep brought on by an unfamiliar place. The knife sang its wolf song beneath us.

Illuminated by the morning sun, the woman inside my mate stood on her hind legs, pacing between bed and hearth, a mortar and pestle in her arms as she grinded wheat into flour. My hackles raised at the strangeness of her scurrying. Her ears didn't perk when she caught me watching; she stood still as prey. The eyes staring back at me were not amber. But still I wanted to pretend all was as it should be.

Hunt with me, I said. She put down her tools and followed me outside, wordless, obedient.

We were clumsy together. I knew nothing about the bow on my back and I longed to drop to my feet and run, to feel something snap between my teeth. She feared the forest and couldn't move without stepping on every brittle twig and autumn leaf, scattering all the birds, who cried their raucous warnings to the deer and rabbits.

She did not deserve the coat she wore.

She might've felt the frustration I left unvoiced as another rabbit scurried away. She leaned her head against me, found the seam on my arm where my fur pushed out against the skin, and brushed her fingers down it. I wondered what she saw—or didn't see—of her mate when she looked up at me.

I'm cold, she said. Let us return home. It wasn't home, but I returned and sat at her table and watched her knead flour into dough. Again I slept beside her, breathing in her scent and the fading wolf smell.

Hunt with me, I insisted again the next morning.

When she followed me into the forest, I ran wild and free as she watched, that she might learn to love the forest as I did.

But it was too much. The skin became loose and fell apart around me in ribbons of shredded flesh. She watched me gather what I could. I feared that, seeing what I truly was, she would flee and I would lose the last piece of my mate with her. But she took me back and sat me by the fire in her home. With needle and thread, she sewed the skin tighter around me.

You needn't worry about losing it, she said. And then she did the same with the fur, binding it about herself until I couldn't see the pinkness beneath.

I stopped trying to hunt the way I used to. We walked the woods until she learned not to fear them, until she stopped hating the cold. When we returned each day to the kitchen table, she hummed a familiar song as she baked and when we laid in bed at night, the knife was silent beneath us. Eventually I put it aside, tucked into a chest of the man's old hunting gear.

It took time to notice that we were neither wolves nor women. We'd become something unto ourselves. Spring came, and she complained about her coat shedding. When autumn drifted into winter again and there was nothing to do but wait for the snow to stop, I kissed the dimpled flesh behind her knees, the same tender place where I might have once snapped a deer's tendon. The urge came to bite. When I did, my teeth were dull, useless. She laughed from deep in her throat.

Hunt with me, she said.

Prix Fixe Menu:
Seared Unicorn Sirloin with Lentil Salad, Butternut Squash Puree, and Cilantro Pesto

(Add Featured Wine Pairing for $16)

Aimee Ogden

*T*ASTE EVERY RECIPE yourself, before you ever try cooking it for others: that's Chef Dave's cardinal rule, the holy writ of Zarzamora's kitchen, and Chef gets what he wants. *I don't want to do it here,* Nina tells him. *Not in front of everyone.*

For her, Chef makes this gentle concession. He hands her a half-pound slab of unicorn meat wrapped in white butcher paper. She still has to prepare it, has to try it; but not in the busy crush of a worknight. "Cook it when Annie is at work," Chef suggests, before the package leaves his hands. Nina shrugs, and he lets go, turning away.

Chef might not have been so understanding, if he hadn't made the first batch himself.

†

THE RAW FLESH is darker than beef, lighter than horse or pegasus. On the skin side, the clinging fascia has a rainbow shimmer in the light from the window—not just birefringence, but true iridescence. There's more fat to trim than you might expect.

†

ANNIE PEERS OVER her shoulder while she peels back the butcher paper. "It looks more like...*meat* than I expected."

Nina sets a pan on the stove and turns up the heat. *It is meat*, she reminds Annie. *Of course it's just meat.*

There's a shriek of evaporating water when the meat strikes the hot pan. Nina's tongue rests on her palate, taking in the seared smell through nose and mouth. Behind her in the tiny kitchen, Annie's hips bump hers. Annie is at the sink, cleaning up the pots and pans and cutting board from the lentil salad that's chilling in the fridge. She prefers the wash-as-you-go approach; she hates when Nina doesn't wash up till the end. Nina *does* always wash up, though. If Annie just leaves it until the meal is over.

Over the roar of the faucet, Nina talks about the time she saw a unicorn. Chef Dave is big on sourcing ingredients, too, and she's been to farms and fish markets all over the state. The forest was different, though. *Just a flash of silver, through the trees.* The bottom of the steak has cooked to a beautiful Maillard brown and parts gladly from the pan. *Like a dream.*

"Didn't you get carsick on the bus ride back to the city?" Annie snorts, and a dirty plate burbles as she submerges it in the suds. "Sounds more like a nightmare."

†

YOU GET DIFFERENT effects, depending on the preparation. Restaurants across the city will be serving unicorn foams, gels, aspics. Chef Dave's recipe eschews molecular gastronomy in favor of simplicity: a seared sirloin cut, a scattering of flaked sea salt, a single narrow V of cilantro pesto bisecting the steak.

At its best and simplest, unicorn meat tastes like your last moment of perfect, complete joy.

†

Annie is not allowed to wipe out the cast iron pan. "I think you love that thing more than you love me," she says, sounding like she is teasing, when mostly she is testing.

Nina smiles and sets out napkins, plates, forks, knives. The pan waits on a cool burner for her attention.

†

At Zarzamora, the dishes are pristine white enamel with a silver band around the edge. These are crisscrossed with a lifetime's knife scars, the edges punctuated with chips. Still, each cut of meat is centered perfectly, bisected with the sauce, a tidy mound of lentil salad on the side. Tucked beneath, three razor-thin slices of beauty heart radish transform into flower petals.

†

Annie pushes the petals to the side of her plate when Nina sets it in front of her, smudging the sauce. "Are you nervous?" she needles. About the preparation, about the forthcoming first bite, about all decisions that have brought her to this table and this moment?

No, Nina lies; she's gotten so good at lying. A deft knife-stroke parts a tender slice from her own steak. She sets it between her lips and closes her eyes.

"What do you see?" Annie is afraid too, of course, though she shows it in her own ways. "Is it—?"

Our vacation. Last spring. Nina's eyes stay closed. *The hawks over the river. The bottle of Frontenac. You looked beautiful in your dress.*

"Good." A scrape of knife on plate, the soft wet sounds of Annie's chewing. Then she's talking, mouth full, about what she sees too, or what she claims to see, but Nina isn't listening. The mists of an old forest gather her in, and across the distance, there is the promise of perfect silver.

WHAT YOU WANT BEFORE YOU KNOW IT

Matt Terl

*T*HE PERSON FROM the precognitive food delivery place shows up unexpectedly. They always do, pretty much by definition.

When the doorbell rings, Dale is slumped on the couch, notionally reading (but with his book upside-down next to him), kinda watching TV (but not looking at the screen), and refreshing social media over and over. It has been a while since anyone rang Dale's bell, so it takes a second ring for him to get up and look out the peephole.

The delivery person looks bored and distracted and kinda cute. Dale has never seen one in person before, but he's watched enough influencers doing the "order precognitive dinner challenge" that the blaze-orange precog food delivery carrier is unmistakable, so he opens the door.

"I've got your food delivery from TelepathEats." The delivery person's thoughtful pale green eyes are at odds with the familiar resigned tones of a gig employee reciting a customer-service script.

Dale can't even finish saying "But I didn't order—" before the delivery person resumes their spiel.

"Of course you didn't," the delivery person says. Their right-wrist Kerch blinks royal blue, so Dale knows they use he/him pronouns, and the royal blue is alternating with a magenta cascade, meaning he identifies as bisexual with a gay preference. His left wrist Kerch is flashing infra-black, meaning *I'm working so please don't hit on me.*

"No one orders from TelepathEats," he continues. "We know what you're going to want even before you do, so we get it here before you figure it out." He sighs with bone-weary exhaustion, and pushes a gray-dyed chunk of hair back over the sandy brown stubble of his scalp.

The ads for psychic food delivery services—the TelepathEats, the Culinaripaths, the Precog Apetits—are everywhere but no one Dale knows has actually used one. Precogs are rare enough that they command insane hourly rates on the gig marketplace, and all of those costs are passed on to the customer, in addition to the usual delivery fees, convenience fees, tips, and other charges. So it's quite honestly insane that this cute psychic delivery guy is standing at Dale's door.

Dale shifts to block the line of sight into his apartment, irrationally worried that even the quickest glimpse of his couch will somehow broadcast how much time he spends there. He fidgets with his own Kerches, royal blue cut with pale pink on one side and silver on the other (at least pretending that he's open to a fling), and, with some effort, makes direct eye contact with the delivery guy.

"I think there's been some kind of mistake," Dale says, and the delivery guy barely stops himself from rolling his eyes.

"That's the major flaw in our business model. But I need you to stop and really think about it for a second: are you hungry?"

Dale, a rule-follower since grade school, stops and really thinks about it for a second. "Actually, I am, yeah."

"Well there you go," the delivery guy says. "I've got your dinner right here."

"That's great," Dale says, "but, speaking totally bluntly to save us both some embarrassment, it would be pretty irresponsible of me, financially, to order psychic food delivery. I really think there's been a mistake."

"Well," the delivery guy says, "that's another really weird thing about this business. Everyone I deliver to thinks there's been some mistake, almost by definition. But, also almost by definition, there never is. Because I wouldn't be here if you didn't want me here."

Dale almost points out that there's a difference between wanting someone here and wanting something unexpected for dinner, but that infra-black left Kerch stops him. Instead he asks, "Okay, then, what do you have for me?"

"I don't usually pay attention," the delivery guy says, "but this one stuck in my head."

Right then, even without any other context, Dale knows with absolute certainty what it is, and says it in unison with the delivery guy: "Grilled octopus."

The delivery guy is nodding, but Dale is physically staggered. He grabs the doorjamb to keep from falling down.

"Whoa, sweetie," the delivery guy says. "Are you okay?"

"I honestly don't know," Dale says.

"Everyone's always weird when I show up," the delivery guy says, "but mostly in a happy way."

"Most of them probably aren't getting an implied death notice with dinner."

"Excuse me?"

"When I was a kid, maybe ten or so, my mom showed us this documentary about a diver who befriends an octopus. It was…a weird choice, I guess, but that was my mom. My dad, meanwhile, spent the whole night talking about how delicious grilled octopus was, drizzled with good olive oil and a squeeze of lemon. I threw a tantrum and swore that I wouldn't be able to live with myself if I ate anything that smart."

The delivery guy smiled. "Very principled."

Dale did his best to smile back. "My dad laughed and told me that it was a dish worth eating, and that if I couldn't live with it, I should make it my last meal. I stormed out, whatever. But my dad was never one to let a bit die, so my whole life, whenever I got upset about anything he'd always say, *Don't order the octopus just yet.* Or something like that. So." He looks down at the orange delivery carrier. "I guess I ordered the octopus."

The delivery guy fidgets with his Kerch. "Are you sick?"

Dale shakes his head.

"Depressed? Do you need help?"

"I think I'm okay. Or, anyway, I don't think I need help, exactly." Dale flicks the Kerch on his left wrist from silver to an inviting gold, immediately tucks his arm behind his back, then awkwardly brings it forward again, rubbing his forearm with his right hand. "Do you know any of the precogs?" he asks.

"They're all at a central dispatch. I'm just a courier." The delivery guy hands the warming pod to Dale. The pod is rounded, expensive looking. It's covered in gorgeous instructional pictograms.

"Do they ever…tell you all anything?" Dale asks. "Give you lottery numbers or anything like that?"

"Nah. There are rumors that they occasionally do favors for drivers they like, but I've never seen it." He looks over Dale's shoulder. Dale, in turn, notices that there are no deliveries left in the orange container.

The delivery guy clicks his left Kerch from infra-black to gold.

"No more stay-away?" Dale asks.

"My shift's over," the delivery guy says.

Having company suddenly seems not only desirable but essential. Dale steps aside and gestures the courier in. Precognition has always been tough for Dale to wrap his head around. Eating something as smart as an octopus still seems cruel, but it would be even crueler to *not* eat it if it's already been cooked. He thinks he's glad he ordered dinner. Or will be glad, anyhow. By definition.

Dale lifts the capsule to his face, one side lit up pink and the other gold by his two Kerches. As the apartment door closes, he inhales brine and char and lemon.

An Unsound Heart

R.S. Saha

"Sick not sick." That's what I always told the healer. The three words, expressed with the cadence of an interrupted heartbeat, left my mouth, vibrating molecules in the air, passing through the healer's protective ward, and finding the groove in their mind that my previous utterances of sick not sick had made. The litany was as familiar to the healer as it was to me.

"Vibrating molecules," I said as they examined my remaining eye. "That's how sound works, yeah?"

"I'm a healer not a scientist." They opened my mouth with a gloved hand. I tried to not taste the latex as they probed my mouth. The gloves were a leftover practice from before protective wards. The Healer's Guild claimed it was tradition to wear them. A symbol of a healer's promise to provide care while still caring for themselves.

I wondered if any healers thought to ask a patient what the gloves represented to them.

"Shouldn't you know how ears work?" I asked as they cast a diagnostic spell. The magic felt like a humid afternoon. It reminded me of what the outside was like.

Unfortunately, there were no spells that felt like a cold winter morning.

"Probably." They shrugged. A stylus scribed my stats onto a wax tablet. "I treat autoimmune disorders. Ear molecules aren't relevant."

I snorted.

"What?"

"Treat." I threw their word back.

Their mouth curled downwards in a wry smile. "Not a synonym for cure."

"Semantics."

"Mmm." They removed my flannel shirt and folded it before studying the stumps my shoulders ended in.

Two more souvenirs from my time as a sapper in the 9th Division during the Vi Colony Wars. As if the unknown autoimmune illness from a healing spell gone wrong and shrapnel to my eye wasn't enough.

The healer nodded at some diagnostic check that I had passed and looked at me. Gray eyes like reticent storm clouds. "You're ready for prosth—"

"No."

"Getting some autonomy back will help, Violet."

My jaw clenched and I broke eye contact. My hair fell over my eye. "I don't need autonomy in a cell."

They tucked my hair back behind my ears. The latex of their gloves rubbed uncomfortably. "Bedroom."

"Is there a difference?"

"Yes. Which is why you're calling it a cell." The healer put my shirt back on me.

The stylus stopped carving into the wax tablet; the diagnostic spell finished its study of me and the healer had read the results. The healer put their things away in a flurry of simultaneous levitation spells. They didn't show any consternation with the complex casting.

"So," I said. "No change."

"No," they said. "No fever. No headache. No—"

"Still can't go outside without my body trying to kill itself."

It hurt less to say the answers to my questions myself.

They shook their head. "No."

No amount of emotional scar tissue could make that word hurt less. Any apathy I feigned was just that. "Sick not sick."

"Yes."

I fell back onto the twin bed, my bare feet still touching the carpet. I curled my toes. "Okay."

"Be right back." The healer stepped into the hallway. The ward shimmered like a mirage as they discarded it. They tossed their gloves in the trash bin behind them.

Sen returned with a tray in one hand and a stool in the other. They sat by the wall in the hallway and balanced the tray on their lap. I looked up at the sound of clattering cutlery.

"First, a grilled cheese sandwich for my lady." Sen bowed and floated a plate through the door to me. The bread had been grilled to gold and toasty perfection. "Made the bread myself!"

"Looks good."

"Beautiful! Word choice, Violet, matters a lot." Sen levitated the sandwich in front of me and had it split along its diagonal cut. Cheese stretched between the two halves like yellow tripwires before tearing completely. Setting one half down, Sen moved the other to just under my nose.

As was silently expected, I inhaled. Butter and cheese dominated the smell but I got hints of the white bread Sen had baked, warm and yeasty. The good hormones—whatever they're called—began going off in my brain and I could almost physically feel their gentle sparks landing on me. Like rainfall.

That same piece was held in front of an ear alongside a fork. I shut my eye and fell to dull darkness right on time for Sen to drag the fork's tines along the grilled bread.

A rough scratching sound tickled my ear and my neck impulsively twisted away. My laugh, a keening sound I hated, broke free with that same impulse. I scowled. "Damn you."

"My services require payment." Sen shrugged and finally let me taste the sandwich. As expected, it was warm, buttery, and cheesy. I got to hear and feel the crunch as I broke through the bread's toasted layer into its soft, airy center.

A bowl of tomato soup arrived next. The worst soup in the world if it didn't have a grilled cheese sandwich accompanying it. I was treated to the same experience with the soup. First, a study of its deep red contrasted with the single green basil leaf Sen had placed in the middle. Then, an invitation to smell its rich aroma of butter, cream, garlic, tomatoes, and…other things. Sen was the chef. I just knew it smelled like the warmth next to a hearth.

Sen didn't invite me to taste the soup by itself. Instead, the sandwich was dipped into it. An acidity enveloped by tanginess melted into the bites. Somehow, the sandwich maintained its shell of crunchiness despite being dunked into the soup.

Little by little, Sen warmed me up until only a little soup remained. They took everything back and held the bowl up to their lips, finishing it with a single gulp. My palate was cleansed by a glass of cold water that they carefully poured into my mouth. Each chilling drop made it down to the subtle heat in my stomach.

"Thank you," I said as they wiped my mouth with a napkin.

Sen smiled and tossed the napkin. They stood, tray with empty dishes in one hand and stool in the other. "You are welcome, love."

They stepped away until I could only see a heel arched up into the air. It settled back to the floor as Sen leaned back to look at me around the doorframe.

"Violet," they murmured, gray eyes wide and misty.

With the lump in the back of my throat and the pressure of tears behind my eyes, I could only meet Sen's gaze.

Storm clouds broke over me as Sen whispered, "I would do this for you even if you didn't need me to."

"Mhm."

Sen, the healer, nodded.

They Commune With the Dead Using Biscuit Crumbs and Wine

Elou Carroll

*T*HIS SÉANCE TASTES like vinegar and grit. Elin believes with every butterfly of her heart. You let her, because it's easier than explaining. She doesn't have the dead cloying in her mouth, the rot of them spread across her tongue like you do.

You've never seen a ghost, but you can *taste* his anger. He pushes dirt and oil between your teeth. He wants her all to himself, even though she wouldn't know he was here if not for you.

And she doesn't, not yet.

Elin is eager—she taps her nails on the bottle, a habit of impatience she's had since you both were little, when it was sippy cups instead of wine bottles. You've already wasted time chatting and drinking and scoffing down your nerves. She is not as patient as you are.

Elin places a hand flat on the wooden floor. "This is where he kissed me for the first time."

Her voice is giddy but it's not the kiss that keeps him here. His death spored in this room—over whispers and biscuits, and later, arguments. It was an argument that sent him out that night. But not with Elin, with you.

If not for you, he wouldn't have been on that road. If not for this room, he would still be alive.

Elin crumbles the Garibaldi—his favourite—in a disjointed circle. She sneaks a currant between her fingers and slips it in her mouth. When she sees you watching she bubbles out a laugh and offers a dried fruit to you, too. Elin presses it between your lips and you blame your blush on the wine.

"You can't touch the biscuits, right? It has to be me, otherwise he might not come?" Elin smiles, and you nod. That's what you told her.

She takes another swig from the bottle before pouring the glass and placing it in the centre of the ring. This is a ritual of your invention but you tell her you found it in a book at your grandmother's house—she had a talent for these things, you said. But you've never needed rituals to commune with the dead.

Elin closes her eyes and grasps your hands. As you watch her, the lingering notes of currant sour in your mouth—he chokes you with tartness, lest you forget about him.

"Hear us," says Elin, loud and unwavering. "We've laid out an offering. Your favourites. Please, come and share with us. We are ready, and willing, to receive you."

This is it.

You squeeze her hands, fingers digging into her wrists, and suck in a gasp like you've not tasted air in weeks. When she opens her eyes, you hold your face in a memorised expression of shock—eyebrows knit just like his. You breathe and squeeze and say, "Elin?"

Pitched lower than usual, the name is all it takes for Elin to rush into your arms, spilling the wine and scattering the crumbs like blood on gravel. Before you have time to change your mind, you hold her face in your palms and you kiss her. He wants to kiss her as much as you do—as you always have.

On her lips, there is no evidence of his haunting.

It doesn't last. When she pulls away, there is a car crash in your throat—metal, oil, fire, skin.

You let your expression drop and slump back to the cold floor. She says your name and you wake for her, feigning a blot in your memory—how long has it been? you ask.

Elin fusses about you but she doesn't mention the kiss. You touch your fingers to your lips and she flushes.

The wine dries sticky and neither of you say a word.

Turducken

Lindz McLeod

Halfway through peeling the carrots for Sunday lunch, Petey announced he'd bred a turducken. The kitchen, busy with humdrum small talk and the chop of various knives, fell immediately silent.

"You mean you've brought one?" Our mother, hands still wet from washing, glanced from the already full oven to my brother and back again.

Petey didn't bring anything. When he arrived two hours ago I watched him stamping through the front door, not bothering to wipe his boots. A trail of wet, orange leaves behind him like a comet tail. Nothing in his hands, not even a bottle of wine.

"No, Ma." He wiped his forehead. "I mean I finally figured it out."

"How in the hell—" Da opened and closed his mouth, searching for words that never arrived.

I put down my paring knife. "How many cloacas does it have?"

Petey scowled. "One, obviously. It was more efficient that way."

Da sank into the nearest chair. "How many hearts?"

"Three. They each need their own. The earlier models didn't survive."

Lunch was swiftly abandoned; we piled into two cars and drove to Petey's house. Past the barn where his lone horse was stabled, we followed him towards a fenced-off enclosure. Despite myself, I was curious. As he swung the door to a little shed open, the pale daylight illuminated a creature only a little wider than an ordinary turkey. The feathers had been shaved away on the front and sides of the bird; strange bulges rippled and pushed beneath the skin, as if it were pregnant. On the beast's back, dark feathers—brown, tipped with cream—bristled against the faint breeze. The tail was a magnificent fan, typical of the species. I'd expected it to look monstrous. More like a frankenchicken. Instead, it just looked like a pathetic, bloated turkey.

"Oh," Da said, sounding a little disappointed. "I thought they'd be on the outside, for some reason."

"Sweetheart, think critically," Ma chided. "The chicken is inside the duck which is in turn inside the turkey. That's how they're cooked, right?" The creature's beady eyes were fixed on my mother and—although they were glazed over—something about its body suggested it was listening closely to every word. She clapped a hand over her mouth. "Wait. It can't talk, can it? I shouldn't have said anything about cooking."

"No, Ma, it's just a bird."

Da stroked his beard. "You're playing God, son. I don't know about this."

"Oh Michael," Ma said, exasperated. "When old Mrs Patterson told us she got Lasik you said she was playing God. When I brought home candyfloss grapes for the first time you said we were playing God. Didn't stop you from eating them."

"I stand by my point." He didn't directly address the grapes, though, so we all knew he'd lost the argument.

I leaned closer, staring into the beast's beady little eyes, watching the red wattle wobble as it jerked this way and that. "What do you feed it? Swans?"

My brother sniffed. "That would be inhumane, Claire."

"You're the one who bred a turducken, bro."

"Children," Ma said. "Perhaps the bickering could wait until after lunch?"

Lunch from Petey's fridge consisted of half a stale loaf and a wad of dubious prosciutto, the origins of which were never verified to my satisfaction; while he'd been dating Ben, they'd usually had a range of supermarket-brand dairy products. Evidently, in-date food was no longer one of my brother's priorities. After eating, if one could call it that, I stepped outside with my mother, who had a cigarette already dangling from her lips. I pulled my smokes out.

"Can I get a match?"

She patted her pockets to no avail. "I could have sworn I put the box right back in my pocket. Here." She took my cigarette and lit it from her own, passing the genetic cherry down the family tree.

I took a long drag, the smoke scratching my throat. "What do you make of all this, Mom? I mean, really?"

"Family supports family, darling. No matter how weird."

"Don't you think it's kind of screwed up?"

"I think," she blew a ring of smoke, "it's a good thing that he's not into drugs and gang crime. And maybe we should just be grateful that he has a hobby."

I stared at the little shed. The head of the turducken bobbed around inside, dipping in and out of view. "Do *you* think he's playing God?"

She considered this. "I think there are worse people to aspire to be."

☦

Bigheart know where food and how to mate. Bigheart know danger, what to peck, when to run and flap.

Middleheart know water. Middleheart always want water—on feet, on body feathers. Middleheart say *fish taste good, paddle feel so good, please water water water please.*

Smallheart has little fast thoughts like eggs cracking. Smallheart know lots. Smallheart say *we* and *think* and *escape.*

Bigheart want to please Man Who Feed.

Middleheart want to please Man Who Feed.

Smallheart don't want to please Man Who Feed.

Smallheart say *danger* and *escape* and *freedom*. Bigheart don't recognize any of those words. Middleheart only think about *diving down, green, fish fish fish.*

Bigheart content to stay inside. Middleheart see pond, want to swim. Smallheart say *now, a chance, man no lock door.*

Three stretch wings wide. Three slide peg up with beak. Smallheart say *yes, that.* Bigheart like outside. Middleheart pulls towards pond. Smallheart say *not yet.*

Middleheart quack. Bigheart feel Middleheart peck inside. Bigheart hurt. Smallheart say *one thing, then bigger pond.* Middleheart say yes? big pond fish please? Please pond? Smallheart say *promise.* Middleheart silent. Middleheart don't know *promise.* Bigheart trust Smallheart. Bigheart say *then what?*

Three approach Man Who Feed nest. Smallheart say *here* and *box* and *fire*. Bigheart peck at box, no fire. Smallheart say, *scratch with claw.* Three lift foot and scratch box. Sparks fly. *Again. Again.* Three watch dry grass catch fire. Three watch red fire wriggle like worms towards Man Who Feed nest. Smallheart say *yes* and *good* and *revenge.* Smallheart say *walk quick, walk now, walk away.*

Three waddle until Man Who Feed nest look small. Three walk until sun hot on feathers. Smallheart say *well done, go further.* Bigheart tired. Three tired. Three walk until no sun. Smallheart say *further.* Three walk until *smell of green, big roar, yellow sand.*

Middleheart say *now pond?*
Smallheart quiet for a while. Smallheart so sad. Smallheart say *yes, now pond.*

ICARIANA

Wen-yi Lee

I FIND HER BY the riverbed after the end of the world, wings tucked under her grubby ribs. Some new kind of being, or else some rich maniac's attempt to engineer homo deux before it all went down. Or went up. Tides, lava, nukes, spaceships. Those last ones, especially, aren't ever coming back down.

I've come across my fair share of bodies, but none of them alive, and none of them winged. She blinks groggily as I carry her out of the scorching sun. Home is a cave dressed up like one. I lay her down on the mattress—she weighs less than the portable generator—and fetch a cup of water.

She sips with puckered lips. She's hollowed out—hungry, exhausted, dehydrated if the fourth cup is anything to go by—but she doesn't look much older than me under all of it. Slim brown eyes and shorn dark hair, roundish face, and of course the wings, spilling from the slits in her dress. They're like grimy clouds across my bed.

"What's your name?"

I don't know if she can speak; her motor control seems fine but—

"Seraphine," she says.

All right, that's a little on the nose, but I'll take it. Seraphine's voice is surprisingly smooth, low and clear like a warning bell. Everybody else—the few there are left—rasps like they swallowed the generation ships' dust clouds. "I'm Kya," I reply. "Let me get you something to eat."

†

SERAPHINE DOESN'T REMEMBER much, but she says she remembers flying. She tries some experimental lifts, but her body crumples before she can get a foot off the ground. Her wings shed feathers that fall mutely as I catch her. "You need to get your strength back."

"Flying," she murmurs desperately into my chest, half-conscious, less a behaviour than an instinct, some immutable part of her she needs to exert over and over again.

"Strength," I reply.

Strength is food. I can scrounge up a decent amount. There's not a lot of variety, but I'm not picky. My goat Mantle does the heavy lifting: cheese, milk, everything silky and creamy. I know where to find cactus and nuts and dates if the season is right. There are dwindling bags of beans and tough grains from the last time I stumbled on a caravan. Water is precious. After her first day, we drink in small measures. These are the blightlands. The sun came too close, and we do our best not to shrivel.

I get used to cooking for two, and to sitting opposite someone while I eat. Seraphine eats like a bird of prey: sharp, tearing bites. Fortunately, she's not picky either. She likes the cheese. I start making more of it.

I show her how to cut open saguaros and scoop out their insides. She's deft with her fingers. I demonstrate how to make nut paste and milk curds. Once she asks, "Is there anything you miss eating?"

Anything with flour. Beef. Carrots. Rice, unthinkable in this dryness. Chocolate. But instead I find myself saying, "Strawberries." Luxurious, sweet things. I had them once as a kid when trade was on its last legs and the growers hadn't yet been packed off past the atmosphere.

"A fruit?"

I wonder again where she's from, what hole she was locked up in. So many things seem new to her. Not the abandoned planet, though; that she never asks about.

"Yeah, fruit." I describe it, and think of Mom. "Maybe they have it way up north still, but it wouldn't grow here."

Seraphine gets stronger every day. I start thinking about going upstream. There's rumors it's less scorched there. That things actually grow. I haven't wanted to before, because I've built too much safety here to abandon for maybes. But now that Seraphine's practically healthy, my encampment seems less safe than stale compared to the way she moves through it. Like my world is too small to fit her. In my quiet moments, I look at her and think we could risk the maybes.

Then one day she says, "I want to fly again."

"Oh," I say.

Somehow I'd forgotten.

†

We stand on the cliff above the caves. There's a decent northeasterly wind, a little cloud cover. Seraphine's tried some jumps and experimental flexes, but this is showtime.

I realise I'm terrified, but before I can speak—I don't even know what I want to say—Seraphine steps off the edge.

The world tumbles, and then her wings snap out and my breath swallows itself. Whoosh and a twist and a laugh and a burst of white feathers arcs past me. Seraphine slices through the air. Her wings burn with the reflected light of the sun, the glow almost harsh.

She circles before darting skyward again. Suddenly she's tiny. Then she's diving again, wingspan eclipsing the sun. But while I'm staring at her, she's staring at the horizon. "I need to fly out further," she shouts.

My euphoria crashes. "How far?"

She shakes her head, half a shrug, face obscured by feathers and motion. "As far as I can go!"

It's a lack of a question that hurts the most.

I want to grab her legs, hold on, never let go. Even if it sends us both plummeting into the scorched earth.

But I don't. I make a gesture that I think means okay. I smile. I let her fly.

Slowly, she vanishes from sight.

Girls with wings were made to soar. Girls with nothing get left behind. That's the way the world works, even after it ends. I make my way back down the cliff. I have so much space, and too much cheese.

†

SEVEN NIGHTS LATER, there's a thud outside. I freeze, slowing on the butane crank. There isn't another sound, but I know better than to trust silence. I grab my prod and climb up to the cave entrance just as a shadow descends.

Even when Mantle bleats happily, I can't bring myself to believe it. But Seraphine is there tucking her wings in as I gape. She smiles like my head isn't spinning to pieces, and lifts her cupped hands. "It took longer to find than I thought."

Strawberries, fat, red, still dewy.

"Where?" my mouth asks, even though I know.

"North," she says. "Just like you said. There's people up there, Kya."

In this moment, I don't tell her about all the times when she was gone that I started thinking about jerky and portable rations. Things I'd have to leave and things

I could bring along to go after her, to go anywhere that wasn't still and scorched. Right now, I just show her how to pluck the leaves off the fruit.

There's only six. Three each. Every burst of juice makes the lump in my throat grow. They taste like somewhere I've forgotten. Somewhere I could know again. When the berries are gone and my hands are sticky, I ask her to tell me all about it.

She begins, "Far up the river, there is a field…"

It's Just a Date

A. Tony Jerome

It's just a date.

I am socially irreparable (no, do better than that, I am possible) and she is extremely pretty and it is just a date. It's okay that my stomach houses pterodactyls at the thought of her eyes on me for longer than a glance.

My mama told me to eat my heart out once. Dinner is at a diner because it makes me feel like we're one of those impossible stories. A story about people alive and loving each other even when the systems work to eradicate them. Sitting in a corner diner booth with her hand on my thigh feels like getting away with something, feels like being brave. It's small but I take my strengths where I can.

It's cold. Even the hot chocolate we shared is turning ice cream in our throats as we walk outside. When I offer her my sweatshirt she says, "Then you'll be cold. How can I be warm if I know you're cold?"

So I give her my hand instead.

For a few minutes, the walk feels absent of fear.

Just holding someone I love while we exist together. She makes a joke and I laugh snort, too happy to even register embarrassment like when I laugh or talk or am in my family's house. She makes me laugh so hard I forget I'm going back to my family's house.

When I catch my breath, I look at her and the breath isn't knocked out of me, it's like breathing learned to do something brand new in my chest just so I could be full body here with her.

"I'm so happy we did this," I say.

She smiles because I'm smiling. She knows my eyes can't hold much all at once, but this, this is something that I want to remember. Her hair plaited back and the little peek of her teeth as she grins, while the clouds shuffle themselves in front of the moon like they need to be a part of this moment too. Her small puffs of hot chocolate breath come towards me so I lean closer and wait for her to meet me where she is most comfortable. I'm happy if it comes as a kiss, or a forehead touch, or a whispered word. Just anything that lets me be near her.

Words I won't repeat hit us from behind. We snap back at the same time and continue walking. She squeezes my hand like don't look back like I'm right here like we're getting home tonight, even if we don't know where home is, we are getting there alive and tonight.

I know she's right. So I squeeze back.

But then, there is a hand that is not kind turning me around and I have not put strength in my heels fast enough to dig into place. I stumble but I do not let go of her hand.

His words blur into the wounding of a playground bully, volume of hurt turned to one thousand; I wouldn't be able to catch them even if I wanted to understand them.

I am terrified and I believe that could go without saying but I want to say it anyway. My teeth have reasons to be sharp but never are when I need them most.

Fear sticks me in place until his eyes slide from me to her.

I shouldn't tell you what happens. I cannot.

There is blood mixed with my hot chocolate breath.

There is too much blood. I cannot tell you what happened. But.

I was afraid and now I am not.

I was empty and now I am full.

The skin that is not mine and not hers makes a home for itself on the sidewalk. When I look around to make sure she escaped—even if those eyes and those hands do not return to me, at least now they have the chance to choose whatever they do next—I'm startled to see her still there. Calm. She looks at me like I gave her an answer she was hoping for.

I wonder if our hungers know each other.

She raises her left hand and I flinch. I'm sorry, but she is patient. When I settle, she lays a finger on the corner of my lips and gently brushes away whatever is left of that person that wanted to hurt her.

The blood in my mouth cakes. I don't think to cry until her touch. The tears surprise me. Fear usually bottles itself and I remain a cabinet for it. I never thought anyone would open me, that anyone would look for the bottle and let it pour itself out.

We hear sirens.

She pulls me until we're running. I don't look over my shoulder. I feel sick and my wings are coming. I don't know where we're going but being with her is enough. There is something—something not covered in blue red lies, something not her—watching me. The eyes make my blood itch.

Mama said to eat my heart out once. But how do I do that when it just grows in the devouring?

I look at our hands, fingers interlaced. How brave she has made me.

Why didn't Mama want me to keep my heart?

The Little Free Guide to Dronewatching,
Abridged & Annotated

Ann LeBlanc

You were the one who watched the drones, not me. You—with those too-expensive binoculars, out alone at dusk, watching their wheeling fractal advertisements against the electric-blue sky. I'd wait, so I could catch a remnant of your too-rare, cheek-aching smile.

Now, I'm the one who sits alone, whose eyes strain to catch a glimpse of swift-sure movement. I'm still waiting for you.

†

Chapter 1: History

[…] In response to the hack, Congress could only imagine a punitive solution. The Feral Drone Remediation Act passed unanimously. Now, it's open season on all drones affected by the Miller-Tesuque virus; aiding them is a felony. […]

†

I SPOTTED A whole flock today, delivery drones, orange paint scuffed and faded, murmurating inscrutable messages against the clouds. I ran out to them, out to the picnic meadow where we had our third date. You were so tongue-tied, so sure I would laugh in your face, as if I wasn't fear-desperate for you to love me. I'll never forget that night, warm beneath the blanket, the softness of your lips, the hardness of your hands.

A few of the drones broke off from the swarm, queuing politely to sip at your charging station. Each one would thank me with stock phrases from their former jobs, like "Thank you for being a premium platinum customer!" Each one, I'd thank back, "Thank you for surviving."

†

Chapter 9: Ethics

[...] It doesn't actually *matter* whether the M-T virus gave the drones intelligence along with freedom. The endless discourse, the detailed analysis of their behaviors, the clues ripped from the guts of dissected drones (and a big fuck-you to those involved in that scene), none of it matters.

Are the drones an insectile hive intelligence? Scripted machines? Punk performance art? Who cares! We must resist the essential human urge to categorize. Whatever they turn out to be, as dronewatchers we make this promise: we keep the miracle going. [...]

†

DO YOU REMEMBER our last conversation, when you called me a coward? And with me up here, and you...well, you were right. I was so mad at you. I wanted you to stay safe up in the mountains, cozy in our cabin. Wasn't our survival, our love, enough resistance against a world that can't imagine queer joy?

But you chafed at the cage safety made of our home. You went down the mountain, to your fucking mutual-aid meetups, passing out bootleg HRT and illegal charging-stations. My anger turned to panic when the police raid appeared on the newsfeed and your deadname was among the arrested. I knew then you wouldn't be coming back.

And now, after months all alone, the part of me that's still angry (and newly brave) wishes I'd gone with you. At least then I could've said, "I love you," one last time. But you were right. I'm too much of a coward to do anything but wait on my mountain, missing you.

†

Chapter 4: Tracking

[…] It's pointless to argue whether RFID is better than QR codes for tracking. Standardization is a double-edged sword. It will slice you open as easily as it optimizes efficiency.

Any tag-and-track system we make standard will be co-opted to capture or kill free drones. Let's keep our mismash patchwork, keep ourselves inscrutable and inefficient. Visibility is a trap. […]

†

Sometimes I wonder if your prison cell has a window. Do you watch the same drones I do? I hope so; I can't bear the thought of you alone.

It bothers me that they fly free while you're trapped. I never loved them like you do. Yes, they're beautiful, but they don't suffer like you do, like I do. Even when their batteries run low, they don't feel powerless like I do, like you do.

I climbed up to the ridge-top last night, watched them flying east into the moon-clad night. They're migrating—like birds—fleeing the wildfires out west, carrying soot-blackened packages from ruined warehouses in their untiring claws. They leave presents on the cabin porch: food, books, toilet paper.

What's going on out there? I'm too afraid to use the internet. Staying off-grid makes me feel safe. Instead I read augury in the flocking of the drones.

†

Chapter 10: Fear

[…] The way people talk about their fear, the way they glance at the sky, reminds me of my mother's terror of the bears that lived in the forest behind our house. The bears don't want to be a danger; they want to be left alone. We are the ones with agency, with power; it's our behavior that makes them dangerous. […]

†

I've made a friend, a drone who stayed behind. She loops above the cabin like a fat orange-striped bee. At first, I was terrified she was virus-immune, here to tell the cops about the drone-helper, the trans woman, hiding alone. But my friend keeps my secrets; she listens to me, shares my electricity, tilts her body up to expose her data-port, a sign of trust, or an invitation perhaps.

Speaking of secrets, I found the box you hid behind the cleaning supplies. I opened it, saw the golden ring, the tiny gem. An engagement ring. Were you going to…?

†

Chapter 6: Help

[...] If you don't have a charging station, cleaning their solar panels can still be a big help. Use non-abrasive sponges and be careful not to introduce water to the chassis. [...]

†

On days when I don't go out—when the weather is too rough for drones, or my fear of spying eyes overwhelms me—I like to read the guide you wrote. I hold the paper version, press my nose between the pages, where some of your smell still lingers.

The drones are doing new things, things not in the guide. My friend has been moving pinecones, making neat piles around the cabin. I've been talking to her, or trying to, through her data-port. I have an idea, but I'm not sure I'm brave enough to do it.

†

Chapter 6: Help

[...] Some argue we shouldn't aid them, that the drones should survive on their own. But humans aren't meant to survive divorced from the help and hope and love of others, and neither are the drones. We must reject calls for self-sufficiency, self-care, and self-actualization. We help the drones, but we have to help each other too. [...]

†

I've uploaded a copy of your guide to my drone friend, along with my own annotations. And even though it might help the cops find me, I've asked her to share it widely among her peers. The world will hear your words—and mine—broadcast from a million airborne voices.

To anyone else listening, I was wrong to wait alone and afraid on my mountaintop. I let my need for perfect safety become a cage that cut me off from the world. Don't repeat my mistake. Listen to the words of the guide: fear is the enemy of love, and the miracle of the drones deserves to be cherished and protected.

But I'm recording this message for you, my love. If you can see the drones, if you can hear them, they'll tell you that you aren't alone.

The drones still fly free. I still fly free.

And to answer the question you never had the chance to ask: I will; I do; I love you.

†

[…] I dedicate this guide to my girlfriend, whose love gave me something to live for, fight for, and hope for. I love you, […]

The Flame Without

Tarver Nova

Landfall +32

JUST A MONTH since we landed here. A month since we made this planet our home. We're here to study this planet, and to study its effects on us. What mutations it gifts. And already I regret it.

My three fellow researchers find this all an idyll. An expedition of endless camping and science. And I can't blame them. This planet is lush from pole to pole: wild-growing indigo plants, sweeping teal skies, and icy-pure rivers. No animals, though the plants' branches curl like climbing fingers in the night.

I can't share their revelry because I've already received a gift: my new vision. When I raise my eyes above the campfire, three flames glimmer from each of my colleagues, just around their heads. Flames.

Ashok's is green, fluffed like a happy cloud. Jacinda's burns a low-roiling, flickering orange, proud like the campfire. Catalina's flame is a purple roar, just like the sass she can't keep secret.

None of them see what I do. If they had, the faces before me wouldn't be so blissful, haloed within their flames.

What does it mean? I cast my eyes to the milky sky. The stars seem to shrug back. Do I see their personalities? Their life force? Their very souls? I can only wonder.

And I wonder what mine looks like.

†

Landfall +36

I'M BROKEN.

We stand in a gently rocking ocean, along pearlescent beaches, and I know this to be true.

The planet's sun—a twin-tailed neutron star—spins high on the horizon. Its plasma trails twirl in a dance that seems taunting: look at you, so hollow, rotten from within.

As we swim in these clear waters, I've realized: their flames are reflected in the water. Their souls, I've decided. Catalina's purples multiply across the waves, prisming out. Jacinda loves to dive, but I never lose sight of her; her oranges flare like a beacon within the deep.

But in my own reflection? There is no flame. I am cold. Extinguished. I have no soul.

This land's vacant blessing mocks me.

†

Landfall +42

ON OUR EVENING expeditions, I've come close to telling Ashok the truth. After all, this is the place for honesty. With our tablets, we scan the plants and rocks along the oceanside cliffs, giving us plenty of time to chat. The sun edges below the waters, its plasma tail spinning above, as if waving us goodnight.

The question announces itself before he asks it. His greens drift low, soften, and then waft toward me.

"Hey," he says, feigning a calm that his flames betray. "You doing all right?"

I make myself smile back at him. "Just thinking about these rocks."

Ashok's flames become tinged with uncertain teal. But he drops it, and we return to scanning the flora.

They'd be horrified to know I see through them like this. See the real them. Their flames give away so much they don't mean to. So much they don't say aloud.

But should I care? I am, after all, empty.

We continue up the ridge. I clear my throat. "Suppose we should get the planet's gifts soon."

Ashok nods, and his features soften. He's decided this is what has been on my mind. He looks to his tablet. "Any day now, I'd wager."

And he treads on. I come to a pause at a wide, unfurling plant. Pretending to study it, but in fact caught with a new, terrible thought.

Perhaps the flames are this planet's blessing, and everyone received them but me. They haven't noticed yet because a sun doesn't see its own light. A fire doesn't feel its own heat.

I move on. I don't want to know.

†

Landfall +55

I'M AN EARLY bird, so I'm seated by the fire, coffee in hand, when Catalina emerges from her pod. Purple flames resplendent. Blazing to outdo the sun. I can't help but wither in her light.

I want to leave. Walk into the woods. Fly off this planet. But we're stuck here. There's no going back.

Catalina must see my discomfort. She comes for me, arms outstretched.

"What's wrong, hon?" she says, her purple flames silent but roaring. I rise, palm outstretched, but my feet are rooted before her.

She hugs me. It's searing, all-consuming. I may as well be face-to-face with the sun.

I'm backing away before I realize I've screamed. The sound dies in my throat and my cheeks flush. I pat my face, my chest, muttering apologies. I'm fine. If anything, I'm lucky the coffee didn't burn me.

She stares at me, agape. Ashok tumbles out of his pod, hair and eyes wild; Jacinda peeks from hers.

I go stumbling for the beach, half-worded excuses on my lips.

†

I SIT ON beached driftwood as the sun pirouettes in the sky. The divide between us is getting worse. Their flames get bigger each day. Only a matter of time before they realize. If they haven't already.

Soft footfalls in the sand behind me. A pause, then Jacinda: "May I sit?"

I consider, then nod. She steps over the driftwood and sits beside me. Orange shades flicker at my periphery, but they're subdued. Almost gentle.

I brace for questioning, but Jace blessedly doesn't speak. We listen to the murmuring ocean for a time. Then, her voice low, she starts to hum. It's a soothing melody, flittering but smart. Hopeful, somber.

Finally, I ask: "What's that from?"

She stills. "You," she says. I blink. Look at her. The orange flames still flutter, though they're gratefully dimmed. "You're such a lovely song," she says. "Did you know that?"

I frown. "I wasn't singing," I say.

"No," Jace says, with the ghost of a smile, "You are a song." She looks out to the ocean. "I received this planet's gift, I think. I hear melodies in you and the others. Isn't it neat?"

I follow her gaze across the icy-clear waters. The waves glitter with the coming night. "You can hear our…songs?" I say. "And what of your own?"

She laughs, gentle. "Now why would I want that?" she says. "Then I wouldn't hear yours so clearly. Listen—"

And she starts to hum the song—my song—again. I listen intently this time. Trying to open myself to it. Burn it to memory. And as it sinks into me, I wonder: do I hear it within myself? Is it there now, echoing, resonating deep within?

My chest feels full, and before long, I feel ready. Ready to share with her what I see. In her, and in the others. Perhaps I have a gift after all.

A Practical Study of Time

M.P. Rosalia

*T*HERE IS NO correct tense to time. Once you've gotten outside of it, there's no way to keep your verbs straight.

This is the first challenge facing any academic looking to study time—practically, of course. If you're sticking to the theoretical, well, then use all the verbs you like; your studies won't have any controls, so you might as well throw accuracy out the window.

I can't keep tense straight here, so I might as well write in present. Everything is always happening, always has happened, always will happen, so I might as well take the middle ground.

Vera laughs at me, when I see her—*when*, what a foolish concept. "Your 'peers' won't ever see this," she says, nudging my elbow. It's hard to feel like anything is tangible, only impressions of feelings, but I can feel her.

She sits across from me in a South Carolina rest stop diner, her motorcycle at the curb outside. The year is 1972, before I've even been born. Her teeth catch the edge of a striped straw slumping lethargically in a neapolitan milkshake, and she taps my notebook.

"You're really keeping a record of all this?" she asks.

There's a date at the top, pulled from the newspaper stand outside, a detailed description of the diner, the waitress, Vera's red lipstick grin. I don't know whether or not the people around us can properly see us, when we meet—*when* is a difficult word—but it would certainly get attention if I kissed the smirk off of her face, South Carolina in '72. Different races, same gender—I decide this isn't the place to test it.

Vera's bolder than I am, but even she looks around like she's testing something. "I can tell you all about this diner. I fucked my ex once in the bathroom. It's *filthy*. You want to record that?"

"No," I said, but I guess I'm recording it after all.

She grins. "He was also filthy."

When I see her next—*next*, whatever that means—it's a bus stop in Kyoto, and neither of us are corporeal enough to be drenched by the rain. No one else seems to notice as she holds an umbrella over our heads. I don't know where it came from or why she has it, considering the rain passes through it as much as it passes through us. She's never had an umbrella before.

"Fancy meeting you here."

I don't know what order she's experiencing "all this" in. I ask her like I've asked her a hundred times—maybe infinite times—to write it down, but on this bench she just shrugs , pops her chewing gum. "Do you know what year it is?" I don't. "It's 2007. There's a crisis in 2008, right?" I nod. "Wonder how many people will lose their jobs," she says, as though it's a game, guessing who among the passengers will be unemployed within the year. My father lost his house—will lose his house. It'll be bulldozed within a decade, replaced with luxury condos.

Speaking in future tense is difficult.

"You're so funny," Vera says on the bus—I don't know how we've gotten on. I certainly don't have any currency that this country accepts, let alone a bus pass. Vera's from Georgia, didn't make it outside the south before she ended up here. She was headed for California, running from an ex-boyfriend who'd caught her kissing another girl—not me. We hadn't met then—*then*, always already happening.

She didn't make it west of the Mississippi.

"You're so worried about linear time passing. Just let it flow, you know?"

I've asked her how long she's been in this temporal slipstream, and every time I get the same sharp-toothed smile in response.

I tell her about my father's house, still standing in Glasgow in 2007, while her fingers trace the lines of my palms. It feels like the only tangible thing that has touched me in a decade, but I swear I saw her yesterday. I remark this to her, and she cocks her head, her braids swinging with the movement and the sway of the bus.

"I thought it'd been thirty-five years," she says, with that same coy grin, and this time I chase it, catching her against the window. The old woman behind us clucks her tongue at us for the public display of affection more than anything else. We're not really here to her—anything she might have to say hasn't even settled in her mind, probably never will.

Vera's eyes are so bright, a warm brown, even in the rain, and the soft skin of her nose is the most real thing I've felt against mine in—

How long has it been?

I whisper for her to stay. We both know there is no here or there, no stay or go.

Do people remember us in the places we pause? Does the old woman remember the girls she clucked her tongue at? I remember her—*remember*, as if it's something that's already happened.

It's hard to tell. Maybe my own experiments are no more controlled than yours, you who are experiencing time front to back, because I cannot return to your time;

I only have memory to go off of and even that's difficult to trace.

"Isn't it strange that we always end up on earth?" I ask, in a shitty club where we can barely hear each other in 2129, and she laughs. She always seems to be laughing. I wonder if that's where time found her—laughing on the interstate, trying to make it west as fast as she possibly can.

"Maybe earth is all there is," she says, and her voice turns mechanical. "Maybe I'm secretly an alien. Take me to your leader, earthling." I almost lose my journal in the hubbub.

Time once found me leaving my apartment in Edinburgh, a stack of neatly graded papers in my bag. I wonder if another me is passing them back, oblivious to the fate of this Steph, somewhere in the stream of time. Maybe there are versions of me that don't get caught by wayward time, looking to gobble up a grad student trying to get past a dissertation committee.

I'm not trying to get tenure. I'm just trying to find a way out.

It's about time I admit that. I don't think I'm meant to move through time like this, out of sync like a bad clock, even if I have someone to find me at the—it's not an ending. It's only a resting place, and even that isn't certain.

Is it alright to say that every time I lose her again, I'm afraid that I'll be left alone here?

(*Here.* There is no here. There's only her.)

She smiles, in another place. "What does time matter?" she whispers. I don't remember my flat in Edinburgh anymore, but I remember the smell of her hair, her cherry red smile, a laugh on the wind on I-10 in Mississippi.

Things don't change here, but they're never the same, so I'm throwing accuracy out the window. I still feel like myself—*myself*, as if anything is permanent. As if I know what that is anymore.

All I know, all I need to know, is Vera, and time.

All the Things I Could've Done That Wouldn't Have Been So Devastating

Phoebe Barton

I could've died of strange lightning, bad wiring burning me to charcoal. Lightning jumps, so we both could've been united in ashes.

I could've screwed up the calculations, accidentally poured my coffee on the control panel, anything that would've kept the machine from firing.

I could've understood your real self before I pushed the button.

†

There were so many choices in the first moments after: stay still as a statue; convince myself it was a dream; take a breath and appreciate a new perspective for however long it lasted. I could've done anything.

You chose to roll over and crush the machine to powder. I chose to scream about how tiny everything was, because that was more comforting than acknowledging how huge we were.

Even then there was still time. I wanted to hold you tight in the rubble, to be giant girlfriends first and figure out the rest later.

I could've calmed myself down and hugged you close so you didn't stand up, didn't flatten half the parking lot under your titanic shoe, didn't see how far away the horizon was now.

I could've done something when you laughed and ran away.

†

The machine could've been made to not work on clothes; you'd have been too self-conscious to run off naked. I would have stayed in the rubble either way. Someone needed to explain why there'd been a laboratory here one second and two giant queer ladies the next.

I was too scared to chase you.

I could've admitted what you were capable of, before you showed everyone.

†

Last week, I still could've stopped you. Instead I lost focus. I escaped into a world that didn't have you in it. I don't know why I held my tears when you yelled at me, or why I called you a…self-centred bitch queen.

Maybe you wouldn't have hit me if I hadn't said that. Maybe you wouldn't have carried so much fury.

†

I didn't want to scare anyone else, so I was careful. I let them poke me and photograph me and stare open-mouthed at me. I scooped up the rubble and flooded the parking lot with tears. I thought you were scared too. I thought you'd come back. I believed in our love.

I could've gone to look for you instead. I could've found you before you found the city.

†

Fights are arguments where fists do the talking. I could've found the right words, talked you down, convinced you to hug me instead. To show me the woman I fell in love with instead of the fists that kept me from leaving you.

I could've convinced you to go to a therapist years ago. To work on your problems. To fill your craquelure with kindness. Isn't that what love is, to hold and to repair?

I did my best, but it wasn't enough. You laughed at me when I begged you to stop. You stepped on a house to see the look on my face. Neither of us knew if it was empty. I could've tried to stop you, but I froze, just like you knew I would. I let you know me too well.

I could've fought back earlier, when our apartment could still contain all your rage. I could've made you hurt when you were still willing to feel.

I could've kissed you with my fist—at least that would've only hurt the two of us.

†

I could've learned how to fight. You gave me enough reasons. Instead our argument stretched gracelessly as I failed to protect the city.

There were so many fields where we could have bit and struck and rolled. The earth would have forgiven us. I don't think the city ever will. Not after you kicked me into buildings and threw cars like stones. Cars with people in them one moment, and viscera the next.

I refused to give up. I refused to let you win. I couldn't. Not when I knew giving up had never solved our problems before.

†

I could've given you mercy, even though you didn't deserve it. One last chance, a kiss and a whisper. Maybe it would've even worked.

I could've been more decisive, plunged that park's steel obelisk right into your eye, so that you died faster.

I could've held the tears that thundered like waterfalls and carried so much blood away.

†

I couldn't let you laugh like that again. So I made sure you never would.

You Who Does Not Exist

AIGNER LOREN WILSON

It's hard to start when you start late, Zyn's voice quietly reminds Helen as she steps into the bar and takes a deep breath. So, this is the dating scene here. What is so scary about this? She'd been expecting a shark tank filled with sexual fluids and bad body odor, but Helen likes the look of the individuals arrayed in odd positions throughout the room. It's as if they are literally trying to put their best foot forward. She is rambling inside her head at you, but you don't mind because if you were real, you would just be happy to hear her voice.

She imagines you prodding her to go chat up someone at the bar, but you would never say that. That's not who you are, that's who she'd always wanted you to be. Instead, Helen sat at a booth opposite two people intertwined at the legs and arms, staring into each other's eyes.

You two were never like that. Helen wasn't the type to sit still and look into someone's eyes unless it was a doctor. And you, of course, hated prolonged eye contact. Sometimes when arguing, Helen would stare into your eyes until you stormed off, angry and skeeved.

Everyone has a drink in their hand except Helen. She's too busy talking to a ghost in her head that is you who doesn't exist. Her fingers play with each other like squirrels on a tree that is her anxiety.

"May I?" a person says, eyeing the seat beside Helen. "How about you take this spare drink I just so happen to have." They hand Helen a tall, skinny glass before plopping in beside her.

You chuckle at the stranger's audacity as Helen squirms.

Helen eyes the cocktail before placing it down on the table in front of her. "I—"

"My name is Hank. He, him, they, their pronouns," Hank says. They've sat down in such a way that Helen only has one way out—asking Hank to move.

Tell him to buzz off, no one says in her mind.

"I'm new," Helen says. "New to everything really. I just got into town today. My stuff hasn't even arrived yet." Helen tries to make it seem like she isn't threatened even though she imagines Zyn chattering about statistics and reviews and how no one cares if you die when you're old, they're all just happy to see you finally at rest.

Hank smiles, flashing high-quality 3D printed teeth shimmering with flecks of gold. He reminds you of an old pimp. "When I was younger, I'd come to places like this and pick up anyone I wanted. The best opening line was always, 'What brings you to a place like this?' It killed every time. Next thing you know, we're knocking things off the wall," he finishes with a wink.

Subtle, you say. Helen laughs. You tell her to hush so that Hank doesn't get any funny ideas, but that only makes her laugh more.

Hank slides their arm around the back of the booth. "Here, everyone is so old, they've heard every smile and seen every lie. And there's only two ways you end up here. One, your partner is dead, and you're alone in the world—harsh but at this age what do you expect? Or two, your family has decided that it would be for the best if you were with others like yourself. Either one is a mood killer, am I right?"

Hank probably doesn't expect an answer, but Helen loves answering rhetorical questions. "Then how do you explain all of these lovely folks having a fine time together?"

Hank looks around at the other people in the room, says, "Why are you so sure they're having fun?"

"Because," Helen says with zero intention of finishing.

"It's a weird sick mind fuck. If they're having fun, that means you could potentially also have fun. It makes it all worth it."

You keep quiet—Helen always said you made it worth it. Even when you weren't there, Helen felt you always. She used to say you made everything better, just knowing you were out there somewhere. Now, she only sips on her drink, blinking away the sudden sting in her eyes. And Hank politely and tenderly changes the subject.

The two continue their back and forth until the attendants close the bar. The real Zyn glides over through the crowd of centurions meandering with their nurses. Despite the small jokes and tender jealousies you keep muttering, Helen says goodnight to Hank and makes a loose promise to see him around.

On the way back to Helen's room, Zyn—the real one—squeezes her arm. "Was it worth it?"

Helen says nothing. She looks to where you would be if you were there, off in the corner of the garden on a bench aglow with moonlight. She thinks back on the ways you met and met again, loved and hated, lived and died. You're not in the garden at all, of course. You're right beside her, like you've always been. But you're not surprised when Zyn wanders off without getting an answer; Helen has always liked not answering questions that deserve a response.

'Sup, Handsome?

Sharang Biswas

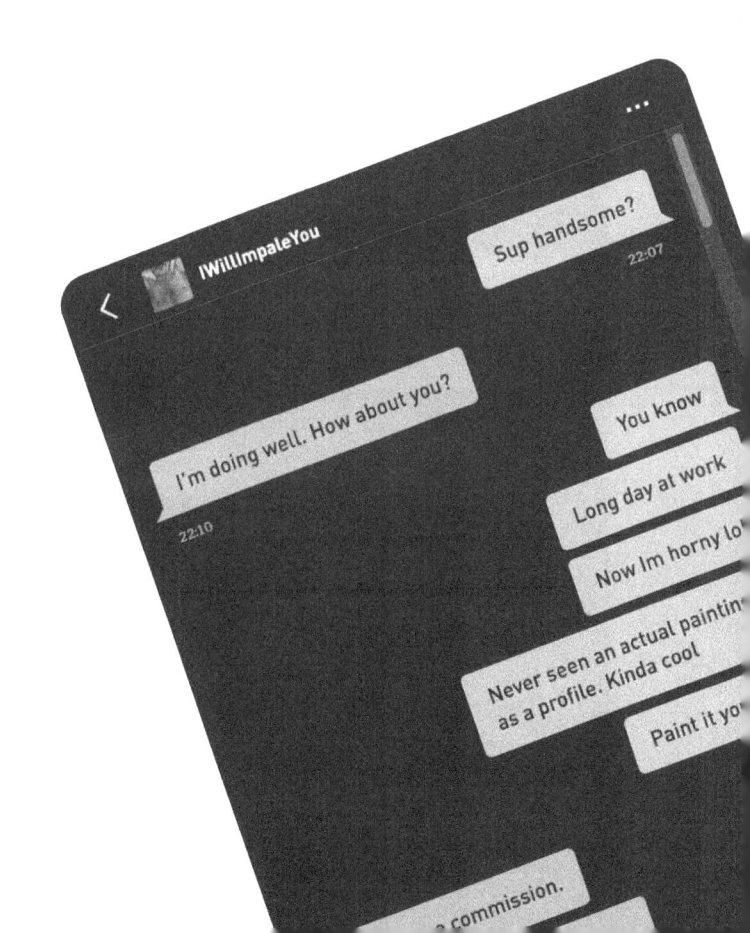

IWillImpaleYou

> Sup handsome?
> 22:07

I'm doing well. How about you?
22:10

> You know
>
> Long day at work
>
> Now Im horny lol
>
> Never seen an actual painting as a profile. Kinda cool
>
> Paint it yourself?
> 22:13

No, it was a commission.

Thanks. I like your profile, too.
22:14

> Got any more pics?
> 22:15

IWillImpaleYou

🫥 you got a drawing of your dick done???

I know a lot of artists.

Wow maybe I should pay someone to draw my dick too 💀

It's an experience. He sucked me off afterward.

IWillImpaleYou

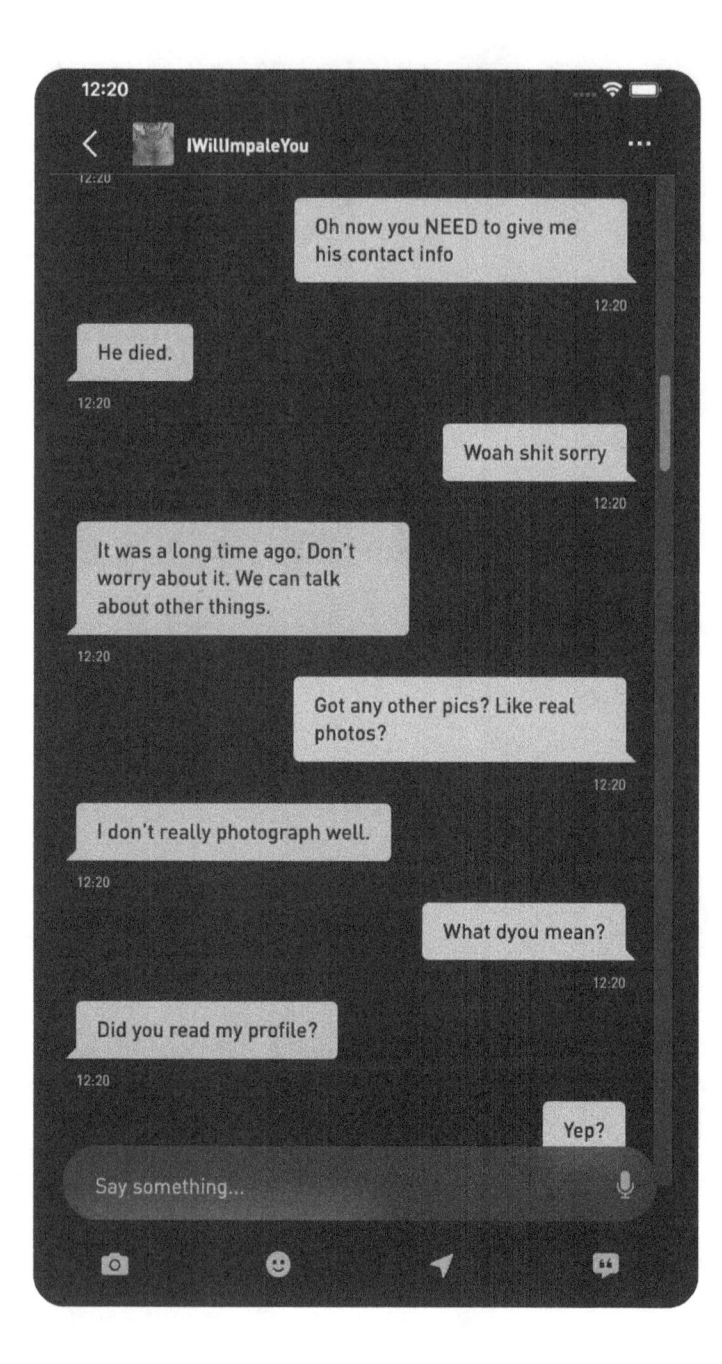

> Oh now you NEED to give me his contact info

He died.

> Woah shit sorry

It was a long time ago. Don't worry about it. We can talk about other things.

> Got any other pics? Like real photos?

I don't really photograph well.

> What dyou mean?

Did you read my profile?

> Yep?

IWillImpaleYou

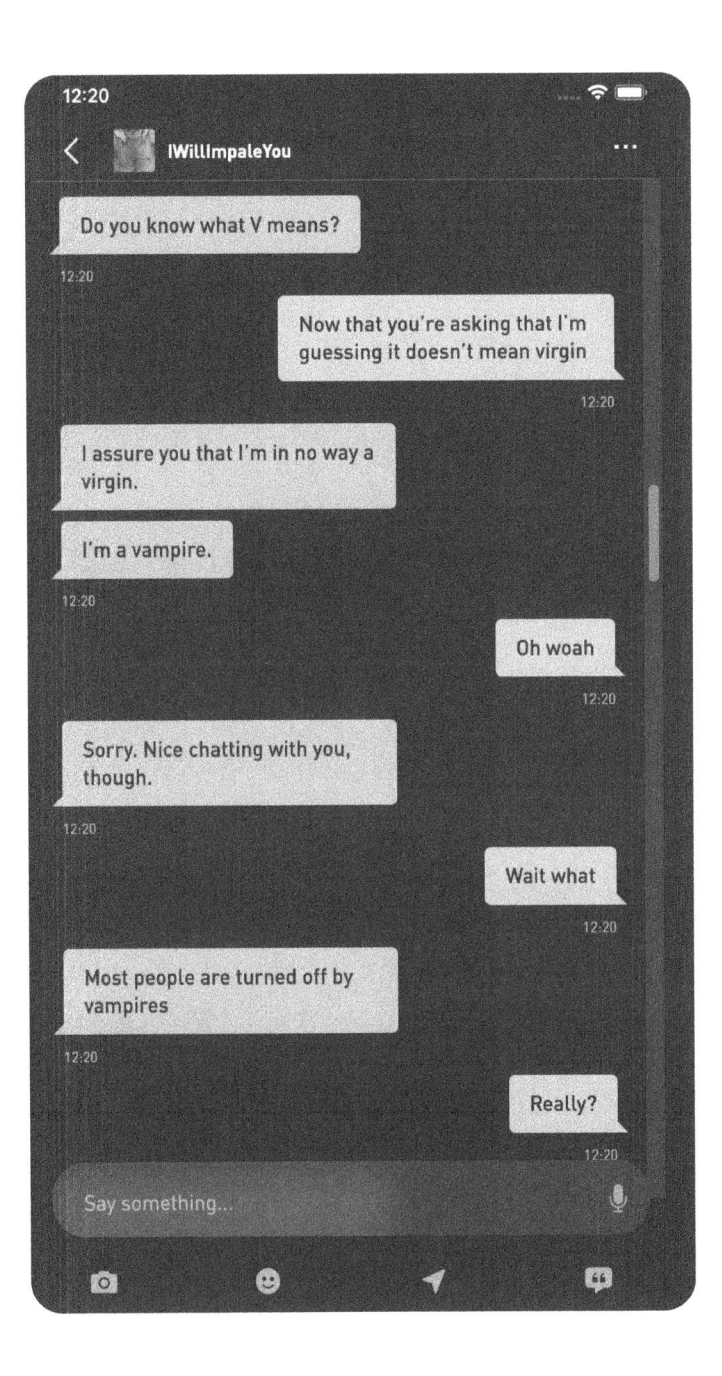

Do you know what V means?

12:20

> Now that you're asking that I'm guessing it doesn't mean virgin
>
> 12:20

I assure you that I'm in no way a virgin.

I'm a vampire.

12:20

> Oh woah
>
> 12:20

Sorry. Nice chatting with you, though.

12:20

> Wait what
>
> 12:20

Most people are turned off by vampires

12:20

> Really?
>
> 12:20

IWillImpaleYou

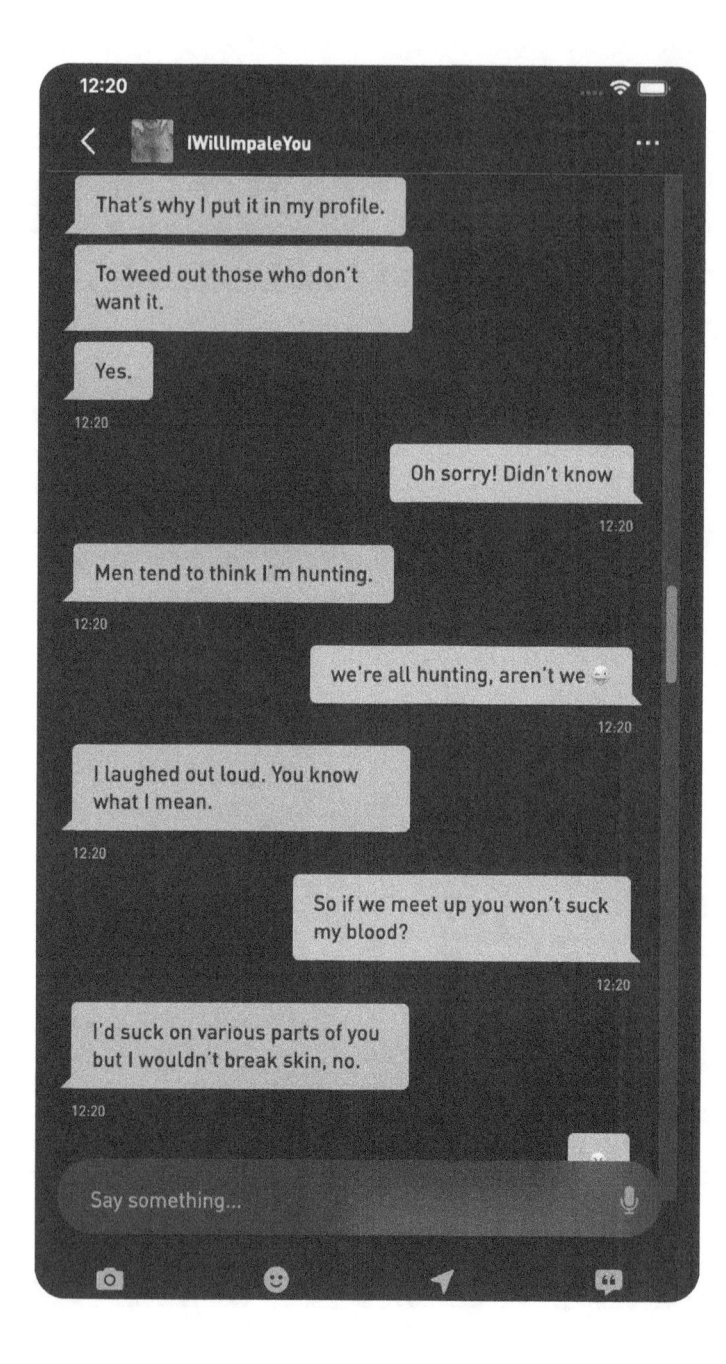

That's why I put it in my profile.

To weed out those who don't want it.

Yes.

> Oh sorry! Didn't know

Men tend to think I'm hunting.

> we're all hunting, aren't we 😊

I laughed out loud. You know what I mean.

> So if we meet up you won't suck my blood?

I'd suck on various parts of you but I wouldn't break skin, no.

IWillImpaleYou

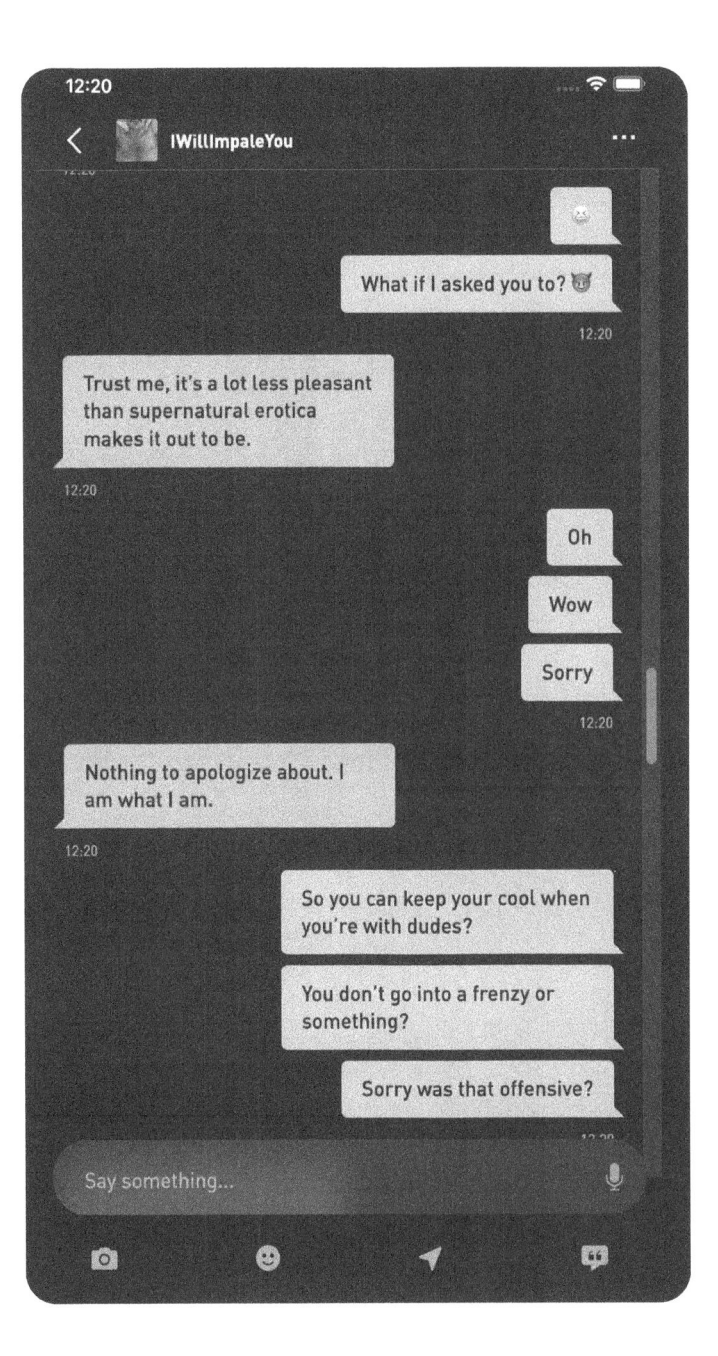

> What if I asked you to? 😈

Trust me, it's a lot less pleasant than supernatural erotica makes it out to be.

> Oh
>
> Wow
>
> Sorry

Nothing to apologize about. I am what I am.

> So you can keep your cool when you're with dudes?
>
> You don't go into a frenzy or something?
>
> Sorry was that offensive?

IWillImpaleYou

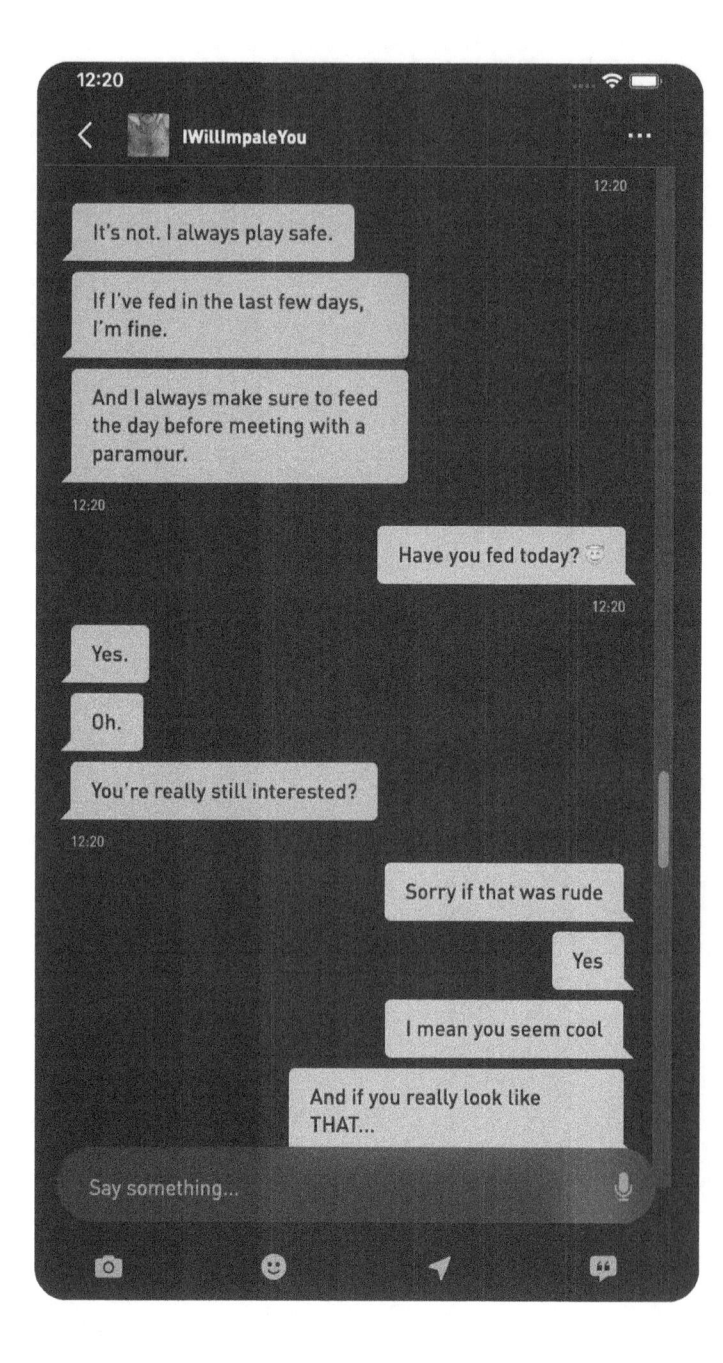

It's not. I always play safe.

If I've fed in the last few days, I'm fine.

And I always make sure to feed the day before meeting with a paramour.

Have you fed today? 😏

Yes.

Oh.

You're really still interested?

Sorry if that was rude

Yes

I mean you seem cool

And if you really look like THAT...

IWillImpaleYou

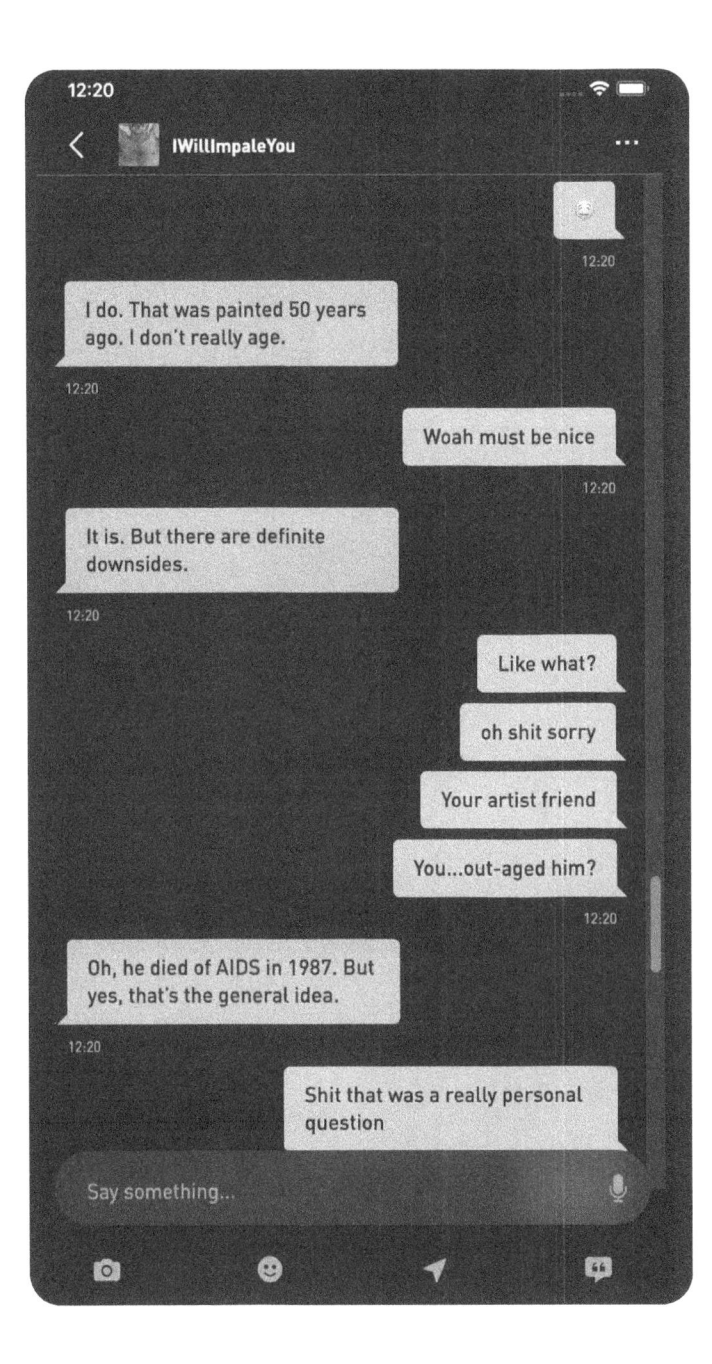

I do. That was painted 50 years ago. I don't really age.

12:20

> Woah must be nice
>
> 12:20

It is. But there are definite downsides.

12:20

> Like what?
>
> oh shit sorry
>
> Your artist friend
>
> You...out-aged him?
>
> 12:20

Oh, he died of AIDS in 1987. But yes, that's the general idea.

12:20

> Shit that was a really personal question

IWillImpaleYou

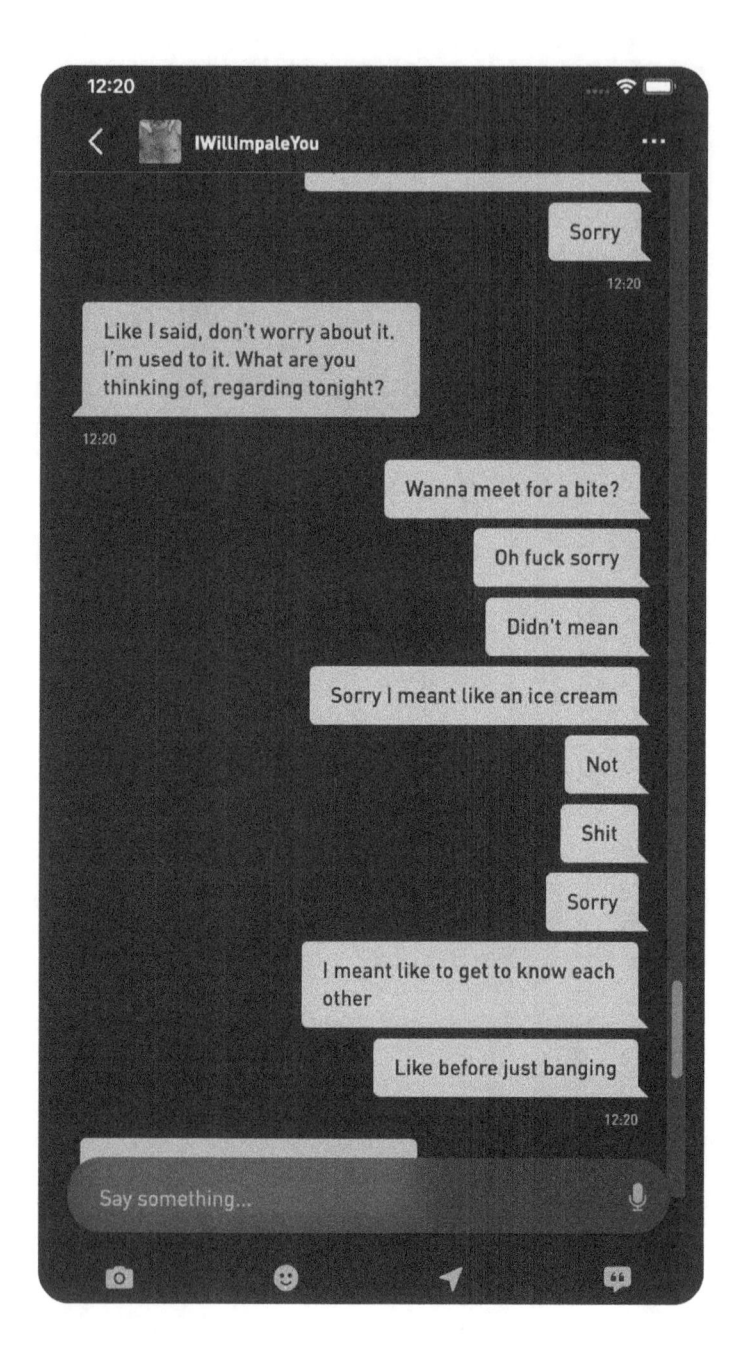

> Sorry
>
> 12:20

Like I said, don't worry about it. I'm used to it. What are you thinking of, regarding tonight?

12:20

> Wanna meet for a bite?
>
> Oh fuck sorry
>
> Didn't mean
>
> Sorry I meant like an ice cream
>
> Not
>
> Shit
>
> Sorry
>
> I meant like to get to know each other
>
> Like before just banging
>
> 12:20

IWillImpaleYou

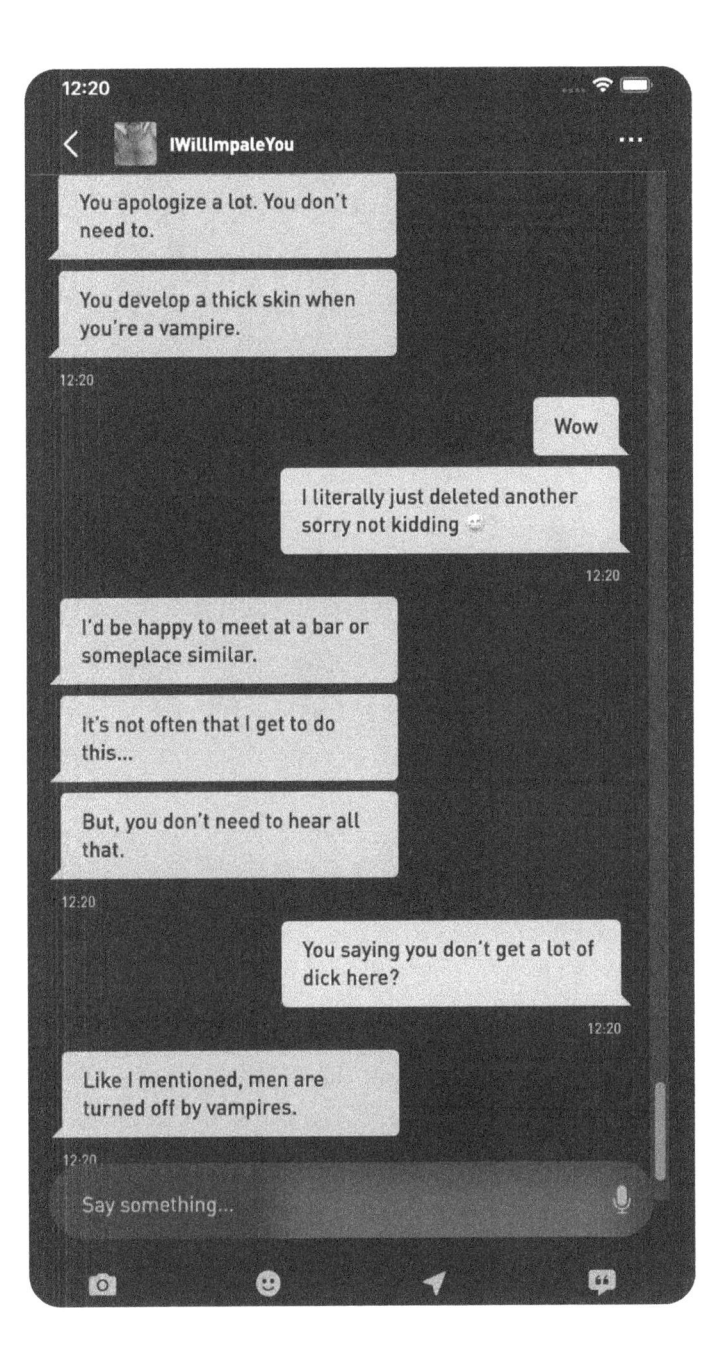

You apologize a lot. You don't need to.

You develop a thick skin when you're a vampire.

12:20

> Wow

> I literally just deleted another sorry not kidding 😅

12:20

I'd be happy to meet at a bar or someplace similar.

It's not often that I get to do this...

But, you don't need to hear all that.

12:20

> You saying you don't get a lot of dick here?

12:20

Like I mentioned, men are turned off by vampires.

12:20

> Like I mentioned, men are turned off by vampires.

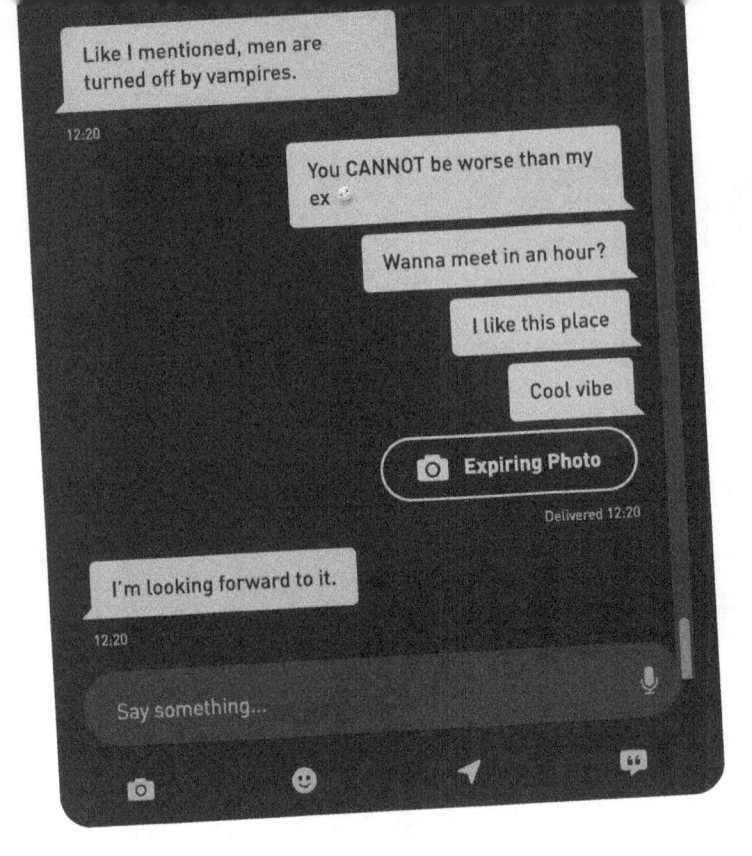

12:20

>> You CANNOT be worse than my ex 😔

>> Wanna meet in an hour?

>> I like this place

>> Cool vibe

>> 📷 Expiring Photo

>> Delivered 12:20

> I'm looking forward to it.

12:20

I set down my phone. It felt heavier than it had an hour ago. "Do we have to?" I asked. "He seems so...nice. And kinda sad."

"Don't tell me you're going soft!" Ayisha scoffed, looking up from her freshly polished crossbow. She applied beeswax every day, *just in case*. "Even if you were gay, that thing isn't even a man. It's a monster!"

Even if I were gay.

"I guess…"

"Hey, if you're *actually* horny, we can bone tonight when we're done." She kissed me lightly on the cheek. "I'm going to get the car. Meet me out front?"

"Sounds awesome," I said, looking away. Even to my own ears, my words seemed clumsy.

Another two guys had messaged me on the app, but they seemed to be ordinary humans. Ignorable, right?

> **IWillImpaleYou**
>
> Sat, 01 Apr
>
> And thank you.
> 23:23
>
> For what?
> 23:25
>
> For not being scared off.
> 23:25
>
> since you sent one earlier
>
> 📷 Expiring Photo
> 23:27
>
> I would very much like to get my tongue on that.
> 23:28
>
> 23:28
>
> Say something...

How to Stay Married to Baba Yaga

S.M. Hallow

1. Don't ask if the pot roast is made from human meat.
2. Human meat is an acquired taste. Acquire it.
3. Collect the eggs the house lays.
4. Crack one into a pan and cook it the way she likes.
5. Crack another into the mortar and grind it down with the pestle. A yolk is not just a yolk: at the bottom of all that gold is a secret only the witches see. You aren't a witch. Choke down the battered yolks nonetheless.
6. When your witch-wife asks you to fetch herbs from the forest, *don't delay.*
7. In the woods, in the dark, your heart thuds and your breath makes ghosts in the starlight. Nothing here will harm you, but when you stand between white pillars of petrified sycamores, you feel the way you did the night you met her, when you were just another Vasilisa, another Yelena, another Marya, another Ivan Ivanovich: another lost soul in a litany of lost souls whose skulls stake the path to her door. Don't ever forget how your story started.

8. Don't lead the girl in the woods back to the hut.

9. *Do not lead the lost girl to your wife's hut.*

10. If you wish to remain married, you *cannot* lead the girl to your wife's hut to become pot roast. You married your wife knowingly, and you have eaten the roasts and the shanks and the bellies and the thighs, but this is *different*. This is the girl you used to be. If your wife doesn't spare her, it'll be like watching yourself get torn apart.

11. When the girl cries after you in the dark—"*Wait!*"—disappear into the shadows and take the long way home.

12. Your wife harrumphs that it took you long enough, and you kiss the snow white hair at her temple. She will use the herbs for spells you won't ask about, and she won't know about the girl like you in the woods. In the morning, wake to the crow of the cockerel house, still in love with your wife.

13. When you stumble into the kitchen and find the girl seated beside Baba Yaga, don't panic. "I saw you in the woods last night," says the girl. "You didn't tell me you saw a girl," your wife says, a smile slicing open her mouth. Whatever you say next, understand that a life and a marriage depend upon it.

14. When the girl says "My stepmother told me not to come home unless it was with light from Baba Yaga's hut," and Baba Yaga asks you "What shall we do with her?" she is offering you a choice. Choose wisely.

15. Assign the girl tasks and chores, the more impossible the better. This is how you proved yourself to Baba Yaga and made yourself worth loving. Order the girl to separate poppyseeds from soil, fish a shuttle from the bottom of a well, gaze upon the skulls of all who came before her and choose where to stake her own.

When she completes all of it, without flinching, make her hunt the firebird and bring back a golden feather. Tell her to trap death itself in a treasure chest inside the belly of a rusalka. Look into her reflection and describe who she sees: the girl she was or the witch she could be.

16. Think of the egg yolk that is not just a yolk. When you look at your wife, sometimes you want to put the yolk back in the shell. She catches you looking and smacks your wrist with her pestle. "It isn't time yet," she says. "Stop mourning."

17. Tell the girl she has passed every test, and she may leave with the light of Baba Yaga's hut.

18. Don't cry when she takes the light and leaves.

19. Sweep the house.

20. Wash the laundry.

21. Gather eggs.

22. Crack one egg.

23. Cook it.

24. Feed your wife.

25. Crack another egg.

26. Grind its yolk with the mortar and pestle.

27. Swallow it.

28. Realize what the girl did to you was a spell: she entered your life and changed it so thoroughly you can never go back to before.

29. Let your wife hold you. Let her feed you. Tell her you cannot believe the girl returned to the family that sent her away to die. Let her pet your hair as you weep, thinking of your own childhood, of your own life as a placeholder in someone else's story, until you

found her, until you made yourself worthy of being chosen by her, until you chose her in return. Tell her you cannot imagine choosing differently. Tell her you would never choose differently, no matter how many times the story is told, no matter who does the telling.

30. Listen: "The light was enchanted," says Baba Yaga. "When the girl's stepfamily beholds it, they will all burn to ash. It was her idea." Reflect: the girl didn't choose people who couldn't love her; she chose to remake the cartography of her world, like you did. Take Baba Yaga's hand. Kiss her fingers. Inhale the scent of spice on her wrist. Wipe your tears with your thumb, and feed them to her.

31. The key to staying married a long time is to know the pattern of the story you've married into. You've met hundreds of Yelenas and Vasilisas, but there is only one Baba Yaga. And inevitably, Baba Yaga is defeated. Inevitably, Baba Yaga dies.

32. Mourn her, even though this has happened a hundred times. When this all started, the woods were deeper with nightmares and dreams. The world ordered itself around a different set of rules. Mourn your Baba Yaga. Mourn the way it used to be.

33. Go outside. The house has laid an egg.

34. Crack it into the mortar and grind it down with the pestle. A yolk is not just a yolk: at the bottom of all that gold is a secret only the witches see, and you may not be a witch, but choke the battered yolk down nonetheless. The moment it takes root, let yourself cry. Remember how she called you a romantic fool and love her all the more for it. Watch your skin harden to eggshell. Feel your heart become yolk. Your mind, your memory, the golden firebird feathers of your stories, all become yolk as the two of you become *one*—one body, two people,

connected at the hilt, a reflection that ripples into an uncharted future. By the time she breaks out of you, a silver-haired and cackling matryoshka witch, you're gone. You haven't happened yet.

35. A Vasilisa or a Yelena or a Marya or an Ivan Ivanovich: these are the roles available to you, each with a story leading you to Baba Yaga's doorstep. When you come knocking on her door, you are ready to acquire a taste for flesh, to separate poppyseed from ash. You will do whatever she asks you to do, not yet aware that you have already done that and more, that she already loves you, that you make each other possible. That is the trick to a long marriage: you must make each other possible. You poured magic into your marriage bond; did you really think it could end?

Darn

Mary Sanche

On a hot day, she can walk out into the coulee and pick the spines of the prickly pear without the flesh oozing for too long. The heat seals up the wound into a clear, bubbling froth, stilled before it has the chance to crawl down to the dust. *Opuntia polyacantha*. Open, prick, poly, ploy.

She makes the eye of the needle with her eye teeth.

Wild rye is good for mending. The rough tooth of the leaves holds well. Like an arrow, once it goes in, it doesn't come out. Not without causing more damage. Same with the spurs of the seeds. Everything is pointed backwards so that forward is the only choice. Further, deeper. In. Foxtail barley will do in a pinch, too.

She has fists full of grass. Her tongue toys the sewing needles, careful, the way she might tongue someone else if she had the chance, but not a lot of people live out here. You're not supposed to put needles in your mouth.

The ironstone cuts her feet but the colour is pretty, red-brown and more red, both oxidizing in the high sun. Breathing.

She lays down on a bed of creeping juniper, recumbent. It's in the name. *Juniperus horizontalis.* From there the horizon looms, lifted by the reaching rills. A rock wren clips across her peripheral vision. Turkey vultures wheel slowly through the molasses of a dense thermal.

The blades of grass peel into strips between her fingernails. The strips pile on her bare belly. Bury her.

Afterward, she bites the chlorophyll out from under her claws.

The first strip enters the eye of the cactus spine. Now she can work.

It's like darning socks. Same concept. Once you know where the holes are, you take a deep breath, imagining the skin stretching over the heel of a wooden egg. Sometimes the holes are hard to see, but she can always feel them. They burn like acid reflux. Like cutting chilis and touching your nose. Like waking up crying. All the little places where men have kissed her, where she wishes another woman would. Every threadbare, ill-fitting ache, begging to be remade in her size.

First, she starts with the warp. Pokes the needle through at regular, vertical intervals, close-knit stripes of rye tugged taut. The closer she puts them together, the denser the fabric will be in the end. She doesn't want too many gaps. It depends on the fabric, though—whether she wants an invisible repair or a strident statement. She prefers the latter. Thick, ropy cords of rye holding her together, barbs flared, wreathed in the warm-sweet smell of decay. It is an art.

Next, the weft. Back and forth, under the first warp thread and over the second. On the next row, alternate. Basketweaving so small she has to squint, all the colour bleached out of her eyes. Her first mending wasn't very clean—stems sticking out like a scarecrow—but she's gotten better. Practiced.

Now, her work is green and good. Tight-knit.

Impenetrable.

When one hole is gone, she patches the next. Her new coat grows, shimmering with silken spurs and the down of silver sagebrush. The juniper berries dye her gold.

The vultures admire her handiwork, and she prowls out from the hills through a fanfare of grasshoppers.

I WANT TO WEAR YOU LIKE A GLOVE

Anneke Schwob

try me on for size (Greenpoint) - w4w

you were sitting with another girl by the McCarren dog park. most people were watching the dogs and some people were watching her but I noticed you. you look kind of like justin bieber? but cuter lol

your hair looked soft. so did your flannel. well-loved. most people dont keep things long enough to love them.

lets see how long we can keep each other around

- do NOT contact me with unsolicited services or offers
post id: 6EQUJ5 posted: 2 days ago

†

YOU WILL FIND us on Missed Connections. A hollow space, filled with loneliness, pulsing with need.

It's 2011. You're twenty-four, living in Greenpoint, and totally fucking broke. Worst of all, you suspect that you might be a total fucking dyke. The gravity of your mundane life will draw you here, to the futon, Adra's legs on yours, faces lit by your laptops' cold light.

†

don't know if anyone even reads these. just thought I'd give it a try.
I don't know what I'm doing.
Hey, are you out there? I hope you're out there.
this is a long shot this is a long shot this is a long shot

†

ADRA'S SKIN PRESSES against yours. Her sense of personal space is capacious. Your hand is so close to the bones of her ankle, the pulse that thrums at the top of her foot. You're in Greenpoint because of Adra, broke because of Adra, so you might as well be a total fucking dyke because of Adra, too.

Adra wonders to your face if you're in love with her. When you fight, she fights dirty, yelling, *Why the fuck do you care, what are you fucking in love with me or something?*

It shouldn't change anything; Adra takes it as given that people are in love with her. She would still be your roommate, still your only real friend in New York, and you would still eat her out in dirty bathrooms, dark bedrooms. Only you would be in love with her while you were doing it, and that would be awful.

Adra only lets you tongue her, touch her, in the dark, and you're not ready for the light. (You will be, in time, and in time Adra will be nothing, only senseless, unmourned meat.) In the meantime, she sits so close to you. In the meantime, your fingers ghost over her thin and tender skin.

Adra nudges her foot into the self-conscious flesh of your stomach. You want to jerk away, and you want to sink into it, and wanting both at once leaves you rigid and trembling while thousands of universes are born and die.

It's not love. It's that Adra isn't a person, but a supermassive black hole. And you aren't a person yet either, just a celestial body trapped inside her event horizon, slowly, inexorably, drawn into her, slowly, inexorably ceasing to exist.

†

you were reading on the subway // we were lost at sea // you were dying, you were already dying, you were dead //
u were buried beneath centuries and forgotten.
We were friends in high school. We were enemies. You were minding your own business.
you were falling through the void of the universe, an unthinking star.

†

I THINK THIS post is about me, you say.
No way, Adra declares. *There's like, thousands of lesbians who look like Justin Bieber. The park's like...their nesting ground.*
Besides, she adds, unthinking and vicious. *You're not even a dyke.*
But it is about you. You understand how it happened, the Missed Connection. Most people were watching the dogs and some people were watching her, and you yourself were watching Adra, too, and that's how you missed it, that's how you always miss it: the moment that someone notices you.
You check to make sure Adra isn't looking.
You click *Reply*.

†

you were wearing a red hoodie. ur hair shown like copper.
You emit no radiation.
sweat soaked ur tanktop I saw ur nipple piercings

You looked happy, you looked awkward, you looked sad. Each of your many arms held a different blade, dripping red. Your legs were perfect, your eyes were perfect. An outside observer can neither become aware of nor be affected by events within your event horizon.

†

BETWEEN THE BADLY-LIT dick pics and misspelled insinuation, we hear your howl into the void. Your pulses and impulses, your thread of hunger. We will follow that thread. We will eat.

hey… you write (tentative, fingers barely moving on the keys). *i think this might be me?*

Hands (thick fingered, blown-out knuckles reading BULL DYKE) rest lightly (improbably lightly, imagine how they might light on you, imagine how hard they might squeeze) on a keyboard.

We'll write: *Are you Real?*

You respond quickly. *Like, am i the right person? should I send a picture?*

Desire pools around your message. You are spread open, like a wound. Other hands (thin fingers, nails dark red like liver) take over.

If you want. But that wasn't the question. Are you Real?

This answer comes even faster: *I don't know.*

†

Let's get ice cream together. Use the sharpest of your knives to take the skin from me and make of it a coat, I will do the same for you. Let's talk for hours. We are binary stars, we are collapsing, you are the black hole at the center of my spiraling galaxy. I want to choke on your cock, your fingers, your foot, your feelings, the memory of your name in my mouth. I'm just looking for friends. I want to meet your friends. I want you to sit on my face. Come away, O human child, come to me, come on me

†

But none of that has happened yet.

It's Saturday and you're in McCarren Park, sticky from Friday's secret, shameful sex. You're wearing your favorite flannel and your hair, yes, looks not unlike teen Canadian pop sensation Justin Bieber.

And Adra is lounging beside you, her hair smelling like cinnamon in the sun. Sometimes you hate Adra for being so comfortable. Sometimes you crave that comfort. You want to crawl inside her, reach fingers and arms and shoulders into the hollows of it and fit yourself against it until you're wearing Adra like a skin. (You can, you must, you will.) So comfortable with everything in her life, except you.

Your hand is right there, palm up, and she won't take your hand.

†

You're still you. Only, lonely you. You don't know yet the violent remaking, the glorious rebirth from *you* into *us*. We are the sculptors of wanting, we are its tailors. You will learn to carve the landscape of desire into flesh, to slip beneath the skin of a body that craves occupation. Yours is the hunger. We will teach you how to eat.

You have no idea what you're capable of.

I'm going to wear you like a glove, you will whisper, fingers on her cunt, and she will pant with desire and then you will, you will, you will. Her cries will become screams as you go deeper, deeper, deeper until you finally sigh, sated, with the muscles of her own beautiful mouth. You're not real yet. But you will be.

Evergreen

Megan Baffoe

Dahlia didn't typically brew from this kind of recipe, but she had no other choice. None of the fabrics she had found so far were *right*.

And the dress had to be perfect.

It was with the fluid hand of a practiced witch that she first added the nettle leaves. These were important: they were the beginning. She had, after all, been gathering nettles when she first saw Cyrene: tall, bow slung over one shoulder and her bounty in hand, a shard of broken sunlight lying across the straight line of her sharp jaw. Dahlia had been slightly curt in asking her to leave the bird population alone (she was the witch of the forest, after all), but intrigued enough by the beautiful huntress to ask her in for tea. Cyrene—with, perhaps, less caution than you should show a mildly offended witch—had accepted.

A ginger stem, next, for the tea that Dahlia had brewed, and two baking apples, for the cake she had served with it. Cyrene had been sincerely appreciative of the skill involved—she clearly held as much admiration for Dahlia's world, composed mostly of the cauldron, the kitchen and the loom, as she did her own realm of string and sinew.

She had a hunter's focus—in some moments, everything stood balanced on the point of her arrow—but she could also see outside of it.

It was refreshing. Despite herself, Dahlia had invited her to visit again.

Now a drop of moonlit dew, for nights spent in conversation, and a winding gold thread, for the quality of it. A preserved water-lily, since their first kiss was by a pond: in her surprise, Cyrene had half-stumbled into it, and they'd fallen. Dahlia could have spelled her dress dry once she got out, but she hadn't.

Crushed coal, for heated words by an evening fire. Dahlia might have watched her leave without calling her back, but she couldn't.

The final ingredient was the ground bark of a tree, evergreen. Not just any tree, of course—Cyrene had proposed beneath this one. A promise, that they would be ever-lasting.

They would be ever-lasting.

Dahlia murmured that intention alongside her enchantments as the contents of the cauldron simmered into paste. By dawn, it was what she had wanted. Tomorrow, she would use this to dye the cloth, already woven, and then she would begin the garment's construction. Cyrene had yet to decide on what she wanted to wear—Dahlia personally thought she would look dashing in a well-tailored jacket—but there should be plenty left over even after Dahlia had finished her gown. The dress would be regal: rich with the colours of the forest, entwined with coils of gold like bursts of sunlight and studded with dew like diamonds. Representative of the domain they had come to share, of their first ever meeting.

Dahlia paused.

It occurred to her that she had something even better for that: a feather, plucked from the bird Cyrene had shot that day.

Dahlia had preserved it out of indignation, then ended up keeping it out of sentiment.

She weighed it in her hands, considering. It was slightly crooked; the animal had slumped to the ground, bent beneath the crush of Cyrene's strong fingers. She had never used a pigeon's feather in a brew like this before, which—especially combined with the complexities of that first memory—might prove ill-advised. Would it affect the colour palette?

Are you still allowed to call yourself 'the witch of the forest' after this? came Cyrene's voice in her head. Dahlia had been huffily putting together an impromptu pigeon pie.

She'd turned, a curt response about hunters and their ill-gotten wares on her tongue, stopped by the brightness in Cyrene's glittering eyes. Apologetic, yes, but not sorrowful; amused, even. From the beginning, Cyrene had been fascinated by Dahlia's strange, enclosed world, so perfect that a dead bird could disrupt an afternoon.

Of course, she ended up disrupting much more than that, and Dahlia had been more than a little fascinated back.

She let the feather drop into the cauldron.

Call Me, Said Kali in Her Black Modified YSLs

Akira Leong

*Y*OU HAD MEANT to get her number.

The moment you saw her, you'd been stricken by her sharp eyeliner. Dark razor-edged wings that made you wish all the lines you tattooed were that crisp. Her cyan ombre hair pulled into a neat updo, waves of her fringe sprayed to look effortlessly in place, her lips a dark midnight hue. The lady was large, taking up the entire doorway to your co-founded brightly-lit tattoo parlour with her hips alone. Even moreso: how she seized the very air you were breathing like she owned it. If looks could kill, you'd be a mangled bloody mess on the cheap linoleum floor from how acerbic she looks.

Guanyin have mercy, she could flay you alive.

You thought she'd want Marcus for his heavy geometric punk-modernist designs, instead you were the one holding the refractal needle gun as you inked in delicate, lithographic white asters around the black outlines of her elegantly polished spinal implants. She asked for the asters to be animated as if swaying in the wind, disintegrating and blooming in perpetual fractals on sepia skin. As unexpected as it was, somehow it was also very her.

She had a humour drier than a Bond martini, "shaken, not stirred," and quipped easily in a rumbling contralto that made you snort unattractively. You thought you might be a little fucked.

That was weeks ago. Marcus still laughed themself stupid when he saw you rushing for the shop's phone because of course you chickened-out and gave her the business card with the shop number instead of your own.

Today was her last appointment; she seemed unperturbed as usual. You reloaded your needle more frequently than needed. Marcus side-eyed your stalling, half encouraging and half those cell aug-pigments aren't cheap. You didn't make eye contact as you added the final touches to the white asters, waiting for your cowardly words to drag themselves from the barbed traffic barrier in your throat.

"You know, getting this tattoo was quite unexpected, Emi Lee." Karishma took out her final payment, immensely pleased. Her cheeks ruddy even without blush.

You had to get her num—

"The first time I walked in here, I only came in to get your number."

ARISTOPHANES AIRS HIS DIRTY LAUNDRY:

A EULOGY FOR LOVE

BASTIAN HART

S UE RIPS OPEN the bag, dumping her soiled belongings on the scuffed floor of the laundromat.

"Some people have no self-respect," says Celia as she watches from over her own folded laundry.

People have their routines. Every week Sue rips through her trash bag, and every week Celia looks over her pristine towers and makes her pronouncement.

But this is Tuesday morning at the Wash-n-Go. Wednesdays, Bernie's there with her three kids, on Thursdays Bill brings his daughter, and Fridays are always a crapshoot.

But on Tuesdays, despite her mess, Sue is quiet. And because Sue is quiet, Celia is quiet. Celia has a lot to say about most things, and while she fights the urge to blurt them out at any given moment, the mutually feigned disregard lends itself to a companionable silence.

(On Wednesdays, *she's an old bitch*, on Thursdays, *she's rude and some people are just like that, sweetie*, and on Fridays? Well, she doesn't quite like Fridays.)

Celia discreetly flicks a particularly scandalous pair of underpants off her loafer. Despite herself, she admires that while Sue brings her dirty laundry in something so uncouth as a trash bag, she insists on taking it home in a different creased and clean trash bag. Celia prides herself on giving credit where it's due, as rare as it is. And, rarer still, is it Sue who's wrenching praise from her arthritic fingers. But watching Sue stuff the bag with twisted knots of clean laundry relieves her in a way. She's glad to see that the other woman had grown a lick of sense after all these years.

Sue kicks off her boots. She peels off one sock then the other before putting them on the pile of clothes that she Never. Ever. Sorts.

Celia rolls her eyes.

"You know," Sue says, interrupting the audible static of radio and road and washer and dryer and the refrigeration of the vending machine, "it doesn't hurt to be a bit nicer."

Celia huffs as she watches Sue unclasp her bra from beneath her shirt, then unimprisoning one arm, then the other, before pulling the thing through the armhole of her threadbare tank-top.

Sue laughs and asks, "Like what you see?"

"Far from it." Celia secretly and not so secretly admires many things about Sue.

Sue's brown nipples are clearly visible beneath her shirt, and whereas Celia has conflicted feelings about her own, as well as the papery skin on her arms, the droop of her gut, and the flatness of her own breasts, she's always drawn to whatever Sue puts on display. But, of course, Sue knows this.

"Come on, live a little," Sue says, wiggling in her direction. "How long has it been since you washed that crusty old thing?"

"As you well know, I wash my delicates by hand."

"I also know your hands aren't what they used to be."

Celia ignores the bait. She crosses her legs and opens her book, the tight ache in her fingers exacerbated by the large hardcover. She desperately pretends to ignore the other woman. Sue is in one of her moods. How long has it been? Celia scoffs to herself. Despite her marriage of many, many years, she reckons that Sue has callers of all types at any time of day. Perhaps she just left one. He or she or they could have dropped her off on their way to the racetrack.

The light in the laundromat shifts, the weight in the air grows heavy.

"Come on," Sue says. And, while Celia refuses to raise her eyes, she imagines Sue—her un-reversed mirror image—shedding the rest of her clothes, her fine lines accentuating an age identical to her own but complemented by a freedom that Celia never affords herself.

Celia is staring at the same word in the same book she has been trying to finish for hours. "Would you please—"

Yes.

Yes.

The text vibrates on the page and the pulp of the paper swells as the ink wisps away like dusty, black pollen.

Y E S hangs in the air.

†

"They say time slows down in laundromats," Sue told her that first Tuesday morning.

Celia had continued folding her clothes as if she didn't recognize the woman's voice, as if the reverberation of those vocal folds were not more familiar than her own.

"Do I know you?" And, as if they never parted, as if they were never split like a sycamore reeling from a lightning strike, she could see Sue's smile, the flesh and blood ghost of that which once smiled behind her.

†

THE DIFFERENCE BETWEEN Tuesdays, Wednesdays, Thursdays, and Fridays at the Wash-n-Go, when it comes down to it, is the company. Celia is not good company, never has been and never will be. She knows this. She also knows that it's not her company that Sue seeks out Tuesday after Tuesday, but a reconvergence.

"There's room for you now," Celia said once. "At the house, I mean."

"I have a home."

"I am not your home."

There was a time when that wasn't true. When their fingers intertwined and their spinal cords wove together like delicate ribbons. When one spoke, the other heard; when one created, the other witnessed.

But now, as their lungs work in conjunction with each other, and their hearts beat in complementary unison, they sit in conversation. Things are different now. Bodies change. Muscles atrophy. Dispositions shift. They align themselves in harmony, one a simple shadow of the other, but now, as it was in the beginning, it's impossible to tell who shadows whom.

†

THE DOOR OPENS; the air is sucked out of the laundromat.

They look up, a beat out of sync, before returning to the book.

Yes.

The word floats on the page in all of its disparate parts.

The stranger grunts at the mess on the floor.

"Sorry, those are mine," they say. Only they can recognize the harmony in their shared voice for what it is.

Yes.

The stranger checks the time on their dryer before leaving again, lighting a cigarette before stepping out the door.

†

THEY REACQUAINT THEMSELVES in bored reticence. Bodies are strange and fickle things, and the millions of microscopic changes made over the course of a week take an eon to cherish and memorize.

They pick up where they left off: Celia entertaining one of Sue's moods, and Sue reminding Celia of all that she had been searching for.

Celia's bra falls to the floor, a respectable nude in cotton and spandex atop Sue's silky lace things. They breathe with ease, whole and unencumbered.

It took Celia twenty-seven years to happen across the right place on the right day at the right time. Twenty-seven years of "just running errands," and "got turned around on the way home." Twenty-seven years of excuse after excuse as she sought Sue out. She lied to the man she married, to her grown children, to every person who cared for the *old bitch*. And now, every week for decades, she and Sue wash their dirty laundry in relative silence, entangled long enough to enjoy the company of one another, until that company repositions itself in space, in that odd little way it does.

A laundromat is neutral ground. Eventually they release one another, sinew unfurling like tendrils, like fiddleheads, like apprehensive embraces. Until they part in silence, Sue with her garbage bag, and Celia with her carefully folded trousers, an exercise in extracting order from the chaos of being.

OF AVAILABLE MATERIALS

Tianran Li-Harkness

When I say I can construct a whole look from a single piece, I mean it.

As a teenager, my driving force was desperation—for something to douse all the wordless emotions inside me and, more immediately, to replace my utter lack of confidence. I got good at mimicry.

That is, until my grandmother sensed I was hiding something, found the apothecary bottles at the bottom of the trash bin. The resulting humiliation was enough. She never brought it up again, except when I came out to her nine years later, and she asked if that was why I was trying to be all those different people.

And, yes, I guess that does kind of explain it. But I don't have to steal anymore.

†

Anyway, this creep—I first saw him while walking home from a friend's place in July, the day's high pushing 100 degrees Fahrenheit. I'd dressed light, but I could still feel my mind frying.

He stood on a corner between old rowhouses, the drugstore and an impassive new apartment building with all the glass, its neon-vested security guards drifting around in a miasma of gentrification. He wore athletic shorts, scuffed sneakers, a red-and-gray checkerboard-patterned shirt and a crisp white cast on his arm. Heat shimmered off the asphalt, and sweat gleamed off of him while the flowers and grasses wilted in people's front yards. He stared off into it all with a dazed, desolate expression.

His eyes slid over toward me as I neared him.

I gave him a little nod. "You all right?"

He looked at me, still all dazed and desolate, just long enough for an uncertainty to waver through me, before busting into the biggest grin.

"Oh, I'm fine," he said. "I'm just fine." His eyes tracked me as I passed.

†

Next time I saw him, on my way to the grocery store, he was still grinning.

I nodded at him again, relieved, at least, to see him looking a little more alive than last time.

He widened his eyes and raised his eyebrows.

"Do you think I'm beautiful?" he asked.

"Sure," I said with all my possible nonchalance, insofar as I think everybody's beautiful, you know? It's no big deal, man. I didn't stop walking.

"I think you're beautiful." He made a loud kissing sound with his lips.

My stomach twisted.

"You want to kiss me?"

I shot him my best bewildered but unfazed look.

"Can I get a cigarette?"

I walked on.

"Hey," he yelled, his tone different now. "Is that a man or a woman? Is that a woman or a motherfucking man?"

He called it out to the street like he expected the sky to answer, or the pigeons. My heart sulked in my chest.

†

NEXT TIME, HE tried to grab at me. I swerved away and hurried down the street. He threw his drink at me, the lip popping off the plastic cup, ice scattering in my wake. My heart thudded like a frog trying to escape my skeleton. I kept looking back to make sure he wasn't following, trying to breathe evenly.

†

I SAW HIM, but he didn't see me, on that same corner outside the glassy apartment building, the rowhouses, the drugstore, smoking a cigarette. He dropped his cig and crushed it with his heel. Something fell from his hand and clinked on the sidewalk. He didn't notice. He turned slowly, and went into the pharmacy.

Passing by the pharmacy, a ring gleamed on the ground, silver, with a small silver skull molded into it. I bent to tie my shoe and scooped it up, an old reflex still kicking after all. I also picked up the cigarette butt, still damp with saliva. Gross, but the truth is, anything you can get helps.

†

THE 7-ELEVEN WAS on the same street where it had been when I was a teenager, and the same witch sat behind the counter. I wasn't sure if they recognized me, but either way, they sold me what I needed without asking questions.

†

IN MY APARTMENT bathroom, smoke swirling from burnt offerings, I held the man's ring, focusing my intention on it. I placed old clothes of mine into the tub and filled it with water. Added the ring with a shake of transmogrification powder—the nostalgic smell sharp in my nose, making my eyes water. Reached in and gave several thorough swirls clockwise, then counterclockwise. I fished it all back out.

My black high-tops had transformed into scuffed sneakers like his. My moth-eaten white T-shirt had acquired a gray-and-red checkerboard pattern. My own athletic shorts were similar to start with, but the texture had changed. Maybe a higher percentage of polyester. I squeezed each item out, hung them on a line over the tub to dry, and drained the water.

†

THE NEXT DAY, I took the clothes down and put them on. I opened the disguise palette from the apothecary and set the guy's squished cigarette butt in the shallow collection chamber. After the palette colors swirled and changed, I painted my face. It went on completely transparent, but when I looked in the mirror, there he was looking back at me. I smiled, and it was his smile. I raised my hands to my face, and they were his hands, his face.

I didn't get far before I found him meandering, maybe looking for another place to smoke, more people to harass—I don't know what other interests he had.

He stopped in the shade of that glass apartment building.

I stopped too, just a short distance away, an exact replica. His wide grin broke across my face. Yeah, it was still a fucking trip. I stood in silence, held him in my sight and waited for him to turn around.

Grown Gown

Derek Des Anges

Camera flashes pepper the rainy evening, and Maggie shifts uncomfortably beneath her clear plastic umbrella. While the stars of the movie loiter coquettishly at the doors, she's stuck under an overhang trying to keep her dress out of the damn rain.

"You'll be the clotheshorse for this evening, right?" Rita had asked, not really waiting for Maggie to answer. After all, who wouldn't want to be seen on the front pages of websites in an experimental mycofibre dress as the face of sustainable fashion?

The rain pours and hangers-on shove her hoping they'd get inside faster. Maggie would claim this one as overtime. Probably.

Once past the cameras, Maggie peers down at the tideline on her grown-gown in dismay, feeling so transparent she was almost invisible. The photographers hadn't asked the right questions; without the explanation, they would just look like shots of simple 30s-style fishtail gown on a recently-out trans woman that no one had really heard of outside of niche scientific publications.

Other guests and press-pass-havers mill about, clutching flutes of supermarket-quality cava; Maggie makes a bee-line for the toilets, resolutely elbowing open the ladies room.

I'm wearing a dress, she thinks, as an older woman in a hot pink suit gives her a slightly confused look. *I belong in here. Stop looking at me, look at the bloody dress.*

The cubicles, at least, are empty.

Maggie flops down on the seat and rests her head on the cubicle wall. The soggy edge of her hitched-up dress falls on Maggie's bare arm. It feels more like wet skin than fabric. She takes a steadying breath. Soon she'll have to go back and explain why she wasn't in any photos—without making it sound like Rita's fault for picking the least camera-friendly, outgoing person imaginable in the hopes of grabbing attention by being Inclusive.

Maggie bumps her head on the toilet paper-dispenser. The damp fabric clings to her.

She's not sure when the walls of the toilet cubicle began to melt, but they hadn't been this faint, shimmering pool of colours before, more an institutional beige with flecks—on the whole this is an improvement.

The tiny, multi-coloured flecks move and swirl, illuminated by an unseen light source and suspended in some sort of matrix. In between them—Maggie railroads her thoughts—something is sprouting.

Microscopic mushrooms spiral slowly up between the flecks on the wall. Hadn't she dreamed of this? The night before she wrote the mycofibre formulas? At least, now it feels like she had.

Mug, says one of the tiny mushrooms in a sweet little voice, like a child.

Maggie pushes her finger carefully against the stall partition. It is still, very much, just a wall.

All that work to save the fashion industry from itself and for what? they ask, elongating stems pushing inexorably between and over the flecks, closer to the surface her fingers could not penetrate.

Rita says we're getting the message out there, Maggie thinks she says, but her mouth doesn't move. She's not sure it or her body can. The cubicle throbs gently, endlessly-twining fungi growing and growing along the walls. Tiny splotches on their surface begin to furl upwards, reveal themselves to be other, even smaller mushrooms. These, too, grow, and grow.

She's using you.

The wet dress stings her arms.

You're using us *but we get proliferation from it. All we want is more of* us. *What do you get from her using* you?

The answer seems to be exhausted and panicky in the toilets of a premiere she doesn't want to be at, but Maggie can't be blunt, or sarcastic. She's not sure those options are open to her now.

Her cubicle shakes as knuckles rap on the door.

The mushrooms pulsate and contract. They explain in soft tones that Rita is a crook; they tell Maggie gently she'll be alright. They spill from the cubicle walls over the floor in an iridescent mycelial tide up her legs, pooling in her lap. All she can do is listen to the way the knocking rolls and thunders, expands to fill all of space and time.

"Excuse me. I was cleaning and—are you okay in there?"

Maggie tries to unpick her tongue from her teeth, realising the cleaner won't communicate psychically like the mushrooms, but still can't find the words.

"Hello? I can see your feet."

Maggie tries to draw her feet up, but it feels like she's trying to swim through mud. Wherever she looks are trails of the thing she looked at last.

She throws out her arm to steady herself—it peels the wet portion of her dress from her skin.

The toilet cubicle vibrates with another tap.

The walls are still. The dress is dull. The walls are beige and black, and all she can hear is the trickle of water from a running tap, distant voices in the foyer, and the impatient sigh of a cleaner.

Maggie opens her mouth, a little afraid now, giddy, unsettled. Nothing spills out: no spiralling mushrooms, no haze of colours. The trip is over.

"Sorry," she gasps.

There's a silence.

Maggie holds her breath. *I shouldn't have said anything.*

Her voice is a problem.

The cleaner will rush off and get security.

It's all going to go to shit, and then she'll have to face Rita as well.

Rita is a crook, comes a murmur. *She's using you.*

Yeah, I know, Maggie says to herself, to the mushrooms. *But that's not my problem right now.*

"Are you okay?" the cleaner asks. "Do you need me to get someone?"

"Please don't," Maggie says hurriedly.

"You stuck?"

"I don't think so."

"Sick?"

"May...be?"

Maggie comes to a decision, clawing her way upright via the toilet-roll holder. Her legs feel like they're someone else's, but she's used to that. A lifetime living in a body that feels like she's piloting it from a distant room makes the dissociative remnants of a hallucination a piece of cake.

It still takes three tries to open the door.

The cleaner—a West African woman in an off-green cleaner's tabard and Crocs—seems to be glowing until Maggie realises that one, she's merely half-blinded by the bathroom lights, and two, she's also a trans woman. Maggie searches for words, but her brain's empty.

"Oh damn, your pupils," says the cleaner, softly. "My sister, you are high as balls. Come tell me what those dickheads gave you."

Maggie looks down at her grown-gown, finally

recalling the instructions she gave Rita. Very clear instructions about not mixing up two similar-sounding Latin names, because one produced an unknown neurochemical in most of its fibres while the other remained politely inert. She'd only ever handled the former wearing gloves, and dried out, before.

With this kind of side-effect, it might be a while before Rita gets her wealth and fame the way she imagined it. Maybe Rita can try the gown on for size, Maggie thinks. Maybe Rita can spend a little time with her own thoughts for once.

But she can't dwell on spite: there are much better answers to be chased after, now she knows what to look for.

"Mushrooms," Maggie says, mouthing the word with a smile. "Mushrooms."

CONTRIBUTORS

Megan Baffoe is a freelance writer currently studying English Language and Literature at Oxford University. She likes fairytales, fraught family dynamics, and unreliable narration; she does not like Twitter, but can be found @ meginageorge. Her published work is all available at meganspublished.tumblr.com.

Phoebe Barton is a queer trans science fiction writer. Her short fiction has appeared in venues such as *Analog, Lightspeed,* and *Kaleidotrope*. A Nebula Award finalist and Aurora Award winner, she lives with her family, a robot, and many books in Hamilton, Ontario, Canada. Find her online at phoebebartonsf.com.

Sharang Biswas is a writer, artist, and award-winning game designer. His fiction & poetry has been published by *Fantasy, Lightspeed, Strange Horizons, Nightmare, Augur* and Neon Hemlock Press. He is the co-editor of *Honey & Hot Wax: An Anthology of Erotic Art Games* (Pelgrane Press, 2020) and recently released *Tome of Dark Delights*, a collection of D&D-inspired erotica.

Elou Carroll is a graphic designer and freelance photographer who writes. Her work appears or is forthcoming in *The Deadlands, FOUND #2, Cosmic Horror Monthly, In Somnio: A Collection of Modern Gothic Horror* (Tenebrous Press), *Spirit Machine* (Air and Nothingness Press), *Ghostlore* (Alternative Stories Podcast) and others. When she's not whispering with ghosts, she can be found editing *Crow & Cross Keys*, and spending far too much time on twitter (@keychild). She keeps a catalogue of her weird little wordcreatures on www.eloucarroll.com.

December Cuccaro is a south Floridian living in the high desert of Reno with her spouse, cat, and two goblinesque chihuahuas. In 2021, she received her MFA in

Creative Writing from the University of Nevada, Reno, and attended the Clarion West Writers Workshop. Her mini-chapbook *The Price of a Feather* was published by Sword & Kettle Press in 2021. She can be found talking about fantasy and fairy tales on Twitter @BespokeChaos.

Derek Des Anges lives inside the internet and writes books. He grows mushrooms, sometimes on purpose, and is currently fighting a losing battle against the number of houseplants in his home. He has been published by Flame Tree Publishing and Tyche Books recently, and continues to resist all pressure to stick to a single genre.

Portia Elan is a speculative fiction writer based in northern California. A Lambda Literary Fellow, her poetry and short fiction have appeared in *Beneath Ceaseless Skies, Ninth Letter, PANK*, and other journals. When not writing, she can be found walking in the hills, visiting the hardware store, or making cake for her wife. You can learn more at portiaelan.com

S. M. Hallow is a speculative fiction author whose short stories have been nominated for the Pushcart Prize, Best of the Net, and Best Microfiction. "How to Stay Married to Baba Yaga" was included on the Locus 2023 Recommended Reading List and selected for inclusion in the *Best of Fantasy, Vol. 3*, edited by Paula Guran. Hallow's other short stories have appeared in *Baffling Magazine, CatsCast, Seize the Press*, and *Taco Bell Quarterly*, among others. Hallow is represented by Laura Zats of Headwater Literary Management. Learn more at smhallow.com.

Bastian Hart is a queer, Black, and mixed-race librarian who dabbles in "The Capital W" Weird. They were raised in a city named after a shopping mall and think body horror is an abject form of self-love. Whereas their day job keeps them somewhat respectable, when they're off the clock they can be found lurking Michigan's wetlands or furiously drafting their monster fucking manifesto. Their work spans the breadth of speculative fiction but ultimately indulges in the novelty of being human. They can be found at bastianhart.com.

Tamara Jerée is an indie author of Black lesbian paranormal romance. Their debut novel *The Fall That Saved Us* won the 2023 Indie Ink Award. Based in Chicago, they use their day job as a bookseller to enthuse about all the weird queer books they love.

A. Tony Jerome (they/them) is a black autistic multidiscplinary artist. A Lambda Literary Young Adult Fiction Fellow, they are a former Lit From the Black! Technical Theatre Fellow, 2024 Roots.Wounds.Words. Speculative Fiction Fellow (Rivers Solomon), 2024 Highlights Foundation Scholarship Recipient, and 2024 Game Devs of Color Con Speaker. Former staff writer at *Autostraddle*, they have work published in *Glass: Poetry, Freezeray Poetry, and The BreakBeat Poets: Vol. 2*. You can find their work at youhavethewritetoremember.net.

Ann LeBlanc is a writer, editor, and woodworker who grew up in the mountains and arroyos of New Mexico, where her story is set. Her debut novella, *The Transitive Properties of Cheese*, is a cyberpunk cheese-heist (in space). Ann is the editor of *Embodied Exegesis*, an anthology of cyberpunk and posthuman stories by transfem authors. Her short fiction has been published in *Strange Horizons, Clarkesworld Magazine,* and *Escape Pod*. You can find her in cyberspace at www.annleblanc.com

Wen-yi Lee is the author of YA horror *The Dark We Know* (Gillian Flynn Books, 2024) and forthcoming adult historical fantasy *When They Burned the Butterfly* (Tor, 2025). Her writing has appeared in venues like *Lightspeed, Uncanny,* and *Strange Horizons*, as well as various anthologies. She is based in Singapore, and likes writing about girls with bite, feral nature, and ghosts. Find her on socials @wenyilee_ and otherwise at wenyileewrites.com.

Akira Leong is a nonbinary dude from Malaysia. Also a queer Christian (still unpacking that). They are currently a postgraduate student at the University of Malaya's English department researching Genre and Manga Studies.They can be found on Twitter @whxyte.

Tianran Li-Harkness is usually not writing and has been trying to learn as much as possible about their local ecology, especially plants. They wrote this story at a time when they felt differently about magic, with love for all fellow shapeshifters of the world.

Lindz McLeod is a queer, working-class, Scottish writer and editor who dabbles in the surreal. Her prose has been published by *Catapult, Flash Fiction Online, Pseudopod, The Razor*, and many more. Her novelette "Love, Happiness, And All The Things You May Not Be Destined For" was featured in the second issue of *Assemble Artifacts*. Her work includes the short story collection *Turducken* (Bear Creek Press, 2022) and her debut novel *Beast* (Brigids Gate Press, 2023). She is a full member of the SFWA and is represented by Laura Zats at Headwater Literary Management. She can be found on twitter @lindzmcleod or her website www.lindzmcleod.co.uk

Tarver Nova is a spec-fic writer and professional night owl in New York. His stories are found with Air & Nothingness Press, *Daily Science Fiction, Kaleidotrope*, and other fine places. He is the assistant editor of *CatsCast*, a cat-themed fiction podcast with the Escape Artists Foundation. Find him at tarvernova.com or show him your cats on Twitter @tarvernova.

Aimee Ogden is an American werewolf living in the Netherlands. Her debut novella *Sun-Daughters, Sea-Daughters* was a 2021 Nebula Award finalist, and her short fiction has appeared in publications such as *Lightspeed, Clarkesworld,* and *Strange Horizons*. Her next novella, *Starstruck*, is coming from Psychopomp in 2025.

Marisca Pichette is a queer author and bone collector based in Massachusetts. More of her work can be found in *Strange Horizons, Fireside Magazine, Asimov's, Clarkesworld,* and others. Her Bram Stoker and Elgin Award-nominated poetry collection, *Rivers in Your Skin, Sirens in Your Hair*, is out now from Android Press. Their debut novella, *Every Dark Cloud*, is forthcoming in spring 2025 from Ghost Orchid Press.

Alice Pow is mostly certain that she doesn't live in a simulation. Her prose has also appeared in *Dragon Bike, Geek Out II* and more. She co-wrote an episode of *The Cryptonaturalist* podcast and is the creator of *Kaiju Cuties*, a webcomic about giant gay and trans monsters. Find her on Twitter and elsewhere as @SummerTimeAlice.

Lina Rather is a speculative fiction author from Michigan currently living in Spain. Her short fiction has appeared in venues including Lightspeed, Fireside Fiction, and Shimmer. Her books include *Sisters of the Vast Black* (winner of the Golden Crown Literary Society Goldie award and shortlisted for the Theodore Sturgeon Memorial Award) and *Sisters of the Forsaken Stars*. When Lina isn't writing, she likes to cook overly elaborate recipes, read history, and collect cool rocks. Find her on Twitter or Instagram as @LinaRather.

M.P. Rosalia is a writer and artist of many forms who enjoys playing with format and writes about gods, identity, and time, and when not writing, prefers to spend time petting cats, climbing trees, and making a mess of oil paints. Rosalia has recently been published in *We Are All Thieves of Somebody's Future* from Air and Nothingness Press.

R.S. Saha is a writer, translator, and editor. Their stories and poems can be found in *The Dionysian Public Library,*

Kaalam Magazine, Unstamatic, and *Strange Horizons*. They are the Associate Managing Editor of *The Maine Review*. Find them on their website iamsaha.com.

Mary Sanche is a queer writer, illustrator, and museum designer living in Canada. Their writing explores the union between science, art, and genre, drawing on their experience working for clients such as Canadian Geographic, Parks Canada, and BC Parks. Their first flash story was published by *Ripe Fiction*.

Anneke Schwob is a former robot impersonator and current writer living in Tiohtià:ke (Montreal). Their writing has appeared or is forthcoming in *Strange Horizons*, *Nocturne*, Flame Tree Press, and *Kaleidotrope*. They can otherwise be found collecting cursed objects, haunting desolate bogs, and online at annekeschwob.info .

Nikolas Sky started out as a romance-writing caterpillar and emerged from his cocoon as a queer specfic butterfly. He lives in the Midwestern US with his very spoiled cat. You can find out what he's doing next on Twitter @ authorniksky.

Matt Terl is incapable of choosing dinner and wishes his future self would do it for him. He lives in Maryland with his family and an annoying dog.

A finalist for the Sturgeon, Hugo, Nebula, Ditmar, Aurealis, and World Fantasy awards, **E. Catherine Tobler** has never won a blessed thing. She has published seven novels with small press markets, and co-edited the fantasy anthology *Sword & Sonnet*. Her short fiction collection, *The Grand Tour*, was published with Apex Book Company. She currently edits *The Deadlands*.

K.S. Walker is a speculative fiction writer from the Midwest with a fondness for stories with monsters, magic, and/or love gone awry. When they're not obsessing over a current WIP or their TBR pile you can find them outside with their family. K.S. Walker has previously been published at *FIYAH*. You can find them online at www.kswalker.net or on Instagram @kswalker_writes.

Aigner Loren Wilson is a queer Black writer and editor of literary speculative fiction. She serves as a senior fiction editor at *Strange Horizons*. Her work has appeared or is forthcoming from *Interzone Magazine*, *The Magazine of Fantasy and Science Fiction*, *FIYAH*, and more. When she's not writing or editing, she's learning, hiking, or loving on her fur babies—both human and animal. Follow her on Twitter @ALWlikeahowl, Instagram @frekihowl, or through her website aignerlwilson.com.

About Baffling

Baffling Magazine is a quarterly online magazine of flash fiction that publishes fantasy, science fiction & horror stories with a queer bent. Stories are first shared online with our patrons throughout the year. If you'd like to support us, please visit patreon.com/neonhemlock.

Visit us online at bafflingmag.com and on Twitter at @bafflingmag.

About the Press

Neon Hemlock is a Washington, DC-based small press publishing speculative fiction, rad zines and queer chapbooks. We punctuate our titles with oracle decks, occult ephemera and literary candles. Publishers Weekly once called us "the apex of queer speculative fiction publishing" and we're still beaming.

Learn more about us at neonhemlock.com and on Twitter at @neonhemlock.